THE
SHOVEL

A
Business
Novel

**Baker
Fore**

&

**Tom
Massey**

Robert D. Reed Publishers   •   Bandon, OR

Robert D. Reed Publishers
P.O. Box 1992
Bandon, OR 97411
Phone: 541-347-9882; Fax: -9883
E-mail: 4bobreed@msn.com
Website: www.rdrpublishers.com

FSC
Mixed Sources
Product group from well-managed
forests and other controlled sources
Cert no. SW-COC-002283
www.fsc.org
© 1996 Forest Stewardship Council

Editor: Jessica Bryan
Cover Designer: Cleone L. Reed
Cover Photographer: Shovel © Tiero from fotolia.com
Book Designer: Amy Cole

ISBN: 978-1-934759-34-9
ISBN 10: 1-934759-34-1

Library of Congress Control Number: 2009925874

*Manufactured, Typeset, and Printed in the
United States of America*

Contents

THE LAWS OF THE SHOVEL

I. Show Up

Show up every day with a shovel, a positive attitude, and a smile. Show others you're willing to roll up your sleeves and go to work with genuine passion for what you do. This combination will open many doors of opportunity for success.

II. Habits Make or Break You

Create the habits today that will produce the life you want tomorrow. Don't leave success to chance—begin today to create the habits that will help you get from where you are to where you want to be.

III. Own Your Actions

Take responsibility for your life by owning up to

your actions without making excuses or blaming others. Be willing to learn from your failures and maintain a spirit of humility in building the collaboration you will need from others to achieve success in the future.

IV. Visualize Your Future

Develop a clear vision of what your future will be and set specific goals to get there. Write these down and take actions to move you closer and closer toward success each day. Remember, a mountain must be moved one shovelful at a time.

V. Extra Effort Pays

Be committed to exceeding the expectations of others and develop a reputation of going the extra mile. When you establish the habit of extra effort, success will be your lifelong companion.

VI. Learn to Love

Begin to view love as a verb rather than a noun, because love is an action. Practice forgiveness for those who fail to meet your expectations, and acceptance of those who are different than you. In doing so, you will move from being a person of success to becoming a person of significance.

FOREWORD

Who wouldn't be skeptical of a man who claimed to have had numerous mystical experiences involving an old prospector carrying a shovel, who he met for the first time beside a railroad track? Yet I knew him for over twenty-five years and can honestly say that he was far from delusional. In fact, he was the most enlightened, fully-conscious human being I have ever met. His name was A.B. Lincoln. He was born somewhere in the Carolinas and was certainly no stranger to hard times or hard work. His life is a story of courage and the determination of the human spirit to overcome adversity. Although he didn't put much stock in luck, he took advantage of good fortune when it came his way.

No one knows exactly why things happen the way they do. Some people are born with tremendous opportunities, yet their lives seem to lack meaning. While others, like A.B. Lincoln, rise from the ashes to lead lives of significance. His parents were very poor and mostly illiterate, especially with regard to creating a safe haven in which to raise and nurture a young son. But you would never know it from how A.B., the man, lived his life. He cared deeply for his family and friends and was passionate about his work. He could speak intelligently on almost any subject, and even though you could sense that he had strong convictions, he had a way about him that put you at ease with your own beliefs.

A.B. was a spiritual man, yet at the same time not overly religious. When it came to such matters he usually let his actions do the talking. That's not to say he wasn't a good communicator, because he was. In fact, he was the most captivating storyteller I have ever heard and he had a razor-sharp memory. As you will see from the stories in this book, his ability to remember and explain even the smallest details of his life (and the lives of others) was amazing. The characters in his stories seemed to come alive as he recollected how each of them had impacted his life in profound ways.

The old prospector appeared to A.B. repeatedly throughout his life and taught him the basic principles necessary to succeed. The old man always used a shovel as the object for learning what A.B. referred to as the "Laws of the Shovel." These laws became instrumental in A.B.'s life, as they have for me and they will for you.

As I write these words, I am fully aware that the stories in this book are a little on the fantastic side— okay some of them may be a *lot* on the fantastic side. You'll have to be the judge as to whether all of them are absolutely true. However, I do believe that while some things might not be scientifically proven, they can nevertheless be true. I confess to you that I desperately want everything A.B. told me to be true, because being a part of his story has touched me in places I didn't even know existed before.

You might read this book and call it a fairy tale— unbelievable or unrealistic. If that's the case, perhaps it wasn't written for you. Then again, maybe it was. Within all people lies a yearning to experience something in life that is fantastically wonderful, even transcendental and magical. Unfortunately this experience is illusive for most people because it lies just beyond the realm of reason and logic. But by the way, so does creativity and love, along with miracles.

Whether you believe A.B.'s story or not, never doubt the truth of the principles the old man taught him. The Laws of the Shovel represent universal truths that are continually working whether we believe them or not, just like the Law of Gravity.

I have gone to great lengths to record the conversations and events as accurately as A.B. shared them with me. This is *his* story. But it is also yours and mine. Enjoy!

—Jason Clark

1

WHEN THE STUDENT IS READY, THE TEACHER WILL APPEAR

Some people say a building is just bricks and mortar. Obviously they've never seen the gigantic building that was the headquarters of the company that gave me my first real job. This behemoth of beauty was nothing but shining steel and reflective glass. Having just graduated with a degree in architecture, I had a rich appreciation for the imposing structure. The tinted glass reflected the sky and clouds as I looked up, giving the impression that the building was disappearing and looming gigantically at the same time.

It was my first encounter with a company as prestigious as Lincoln Construction, and this increased my anxiety about making a good first impression on my new boss. I entered through the revolving doors and did what I'm sure all first time visitors do. I stared up at the glass ceiling over two hundred feet high.

Before getting on the elevator, I stopped at the men's room to comb what was left of my recently-cut hair. As part of my efforts to create a good impression, I had let the barber cut my curly black hair much too short. It made me look even younger than I was—hardly old enough to be a college graduate. After smoothing my tie and the wrinkles in my used but still serviceable suit, I looked in the mirror and decided I was presentable.

The ride in the glass elevator was spectacular, and as I stepped off into a pleasant reception area filled with cushy leather chairs I wondered why a man as successful as A. B. Lincoln wanted to meet with a new and inexperienced, lower level employee. The receptionist looked up from her keyboard and flashed me a genuine smile.

"Good morning. My name is Jason Clark," I said.

"Welcome, Mr. Clark. Mr. Lincoln has several appointments this morning and asked that you make yourself comfortable in your new office one floor below. And do feel free to wander the building and familiarize yourself with the various facilities we enjoy here. There is a map of the building on your desk and your name is already on the door. I don't think you'll have any problems finding your way around, but if you do just ask someone or call me. My name is Ann Miller. Mr. Lincoln would like you to join him for lunch here at noon. Be on time and try to relax a little. You are going to do fine."

Amazed at her perception of the nervousness I was trying so hard to hide, I smiled back and simply said, "What's your extension number?"

"My extension is 2677. That is BOSS on your phone if you forget. I answer his phone, get it?" She laughed. I got it and somehow her obvious amusement at something so silly helped me relax a little.

I took the elevator back down one floor and stepped off into a large room filled with tables laden with models of buildings of assorted designs and in various stages of completion. They seemed to be works in progress. Around this room were offices backed against the outer walls of glass. The front of each office was glass as well. In each office the opposing side walls were paneled with rich mahogany wood. One wall was covered with pictures—the opposite wall simply had a gold shovel hanging on it.

Hmmm... very interesting, I thought. Why a shovel?

There was a central conference room straight across from the elevator and several people were seated around a long table. One office had the door shut with my name gleaming from a brass strip. I entered my new office and immediately noticed that both walls were bare. I sat at my desk and swiveled around to look out across the skyline of the city. If the number of models on the tables represented company projects, I had a hunch that this was a view I might not spend much time enjoying because of my busy work schedule. I unpacked one framed diploma and two photographs from my briefcase, one of Mom and one of my little sister. My desk was set. I could hang the diploma on the wall later.

According to the directory on my desk, each floor was designated by specific department and its various functions, along with the names and extensions numbers of the respective staff members. The second floor entry said "Cafeteria" and the third floor was simply labeled "Health and Fitness." I decided to take a quick a tour before the meeting with the boss. The Cafeteria was clean and modern, as I expected. However, when I stepped off the elevator on the third floor I was surprised to find a fully-equipped weight room with treadmills, stationary bicycles, and stair-climbing machines—in addition to an activity room for aerobic and yoga classes, a couple of racquetball courts, and separate locker rooms for women and men. Mr. Lincoln obviously believed that healthy activities were important for his associates.

I checked my watch and discovered that the morning had slipped by quickly while I was exploring. So I hopped on the elevator and went back up to the top floor. Once again Ann's warm smile greeted me.

"I'm glad you came back early. Mr. Lincoln has asked me to cancel his appointments for the rest of the afternoon so he can spend ample time with you on your first day. He will see you now, so go right on in."

The first thing I noticed as I entered Mr. Lincoln's office was another shovel, only this one was not on the wall—it was standing in the corner behind his desk. Unlike the gold ones on the walls of the other offices, this shovel was old and obviously well used. Mr. Lincoln bounded out of his chair from behind a massive desk, which held only a couple of papers lying on a blotter. He was trim and athletic looking, and wearing a tailored suit with a loosely buttoned denim shirt that matched the color of his eyes. He had a big smile and firm handshake that immediately made me feel as if he was genuinely glad to meet me. He looked me square in the eyes when he spoke, as if nothing else in the world mattered to him but me and our conversation.

"Well, did you bring your shovel?" he said.

"No, sir, but I have noticed there seems to be no shortage of them around here."

His laughter was infectious and again his smile put me at ease. "Shovels are very important in the construction business. In fact, a shovel saved my life and it has been the backbone of this company from its beginning. Have a seat and I'll explain to you why it will be important in your life, too."

I turned and sat down in one of two large comfortable chairs facing each other. Mr. Lincoln sat down across from me. "The gold shovels you've seen hanging on the walls are the ones I have given to our associates. Each of them has the same words etched on the blade as that old shovel standing there. I call these words the 'Laws of the Shovel' because, like the Law of Gravity, you can always trust them to work."

Then he pointed toward the corner of his office. "That old shovel over there was given to me many years ago when my life was much different than it is today.

A.B. TELLS JASON ABOUT HIS FAMILY, AND WHAT HAPPENED WHEN HE MET THE OLD PROSPECTOR

My father was an alcoholic and my mother died when I was a young boy. I dropped out of school and left home to get away from my abusive father. I slept in abandoned cars, and when the weather was nice enough I slept under the stars behind a warehouse over by the old railroad tracks on the south end of town.

One night I was sitting by a fire of scrap wood warming a can of beans for my dinner. I looked up and was surprised to see an old man walking down the railroad tracks toward me. He was leading a donkey that had a pack on its back—a pick and a couple of shovels were tied to the pack, and I thought he might be a prospector. The old man had a long gray beard and dusty clothes topped by an over-sized, weather-beaten cowboy hat. His face was leathered and wrinkled but he had a large, almost captivating smile.

At first I thought he was going to keep walking, but when he was directly in front of me he stopped and stepped off the tracks and led his donkey over to my fire. He let go of the donkey's halter and slipped the pack from its back, letting it drop to the ground. Then he sat down next to it and looked across the fire at me. He took a couple of tin plates and two forks from the pack and handed them to me, saying, "Well, A. B., you going to just sit there, or are you going to share some of those beans with me?"

I reached for the beans and poured about half onto each plate, thinking to myself: *How does this old coot know my name?*

He took the plate from my hand, and as if he could read my mind, he said, "Thanks, son. By the way, I know your name because I have been watching you for a long time."

Looking into his eyes I realized I was not afraid of him. This surprised me. For some reason his words were calming. We sat by the fire and ate the beans together in silence. Occasionally he would raise his eyes from his plate and look into my eyes, and I felt as if he was looking right down into my soul.

"I know where I'm going to be tomorrow morning and the people I must see," he said. "What about you?"

I thought about what I'd be doing tomorrow, and it was probably not going to be any different than yesterday or today. More than likely I'd be hanging out with Buddy and the other guys. I felt accepted when I was with them. They didn't look down on me like the rich little snobs who lived on their daddy's money in their fancy houses. Buddy and the guys treated me like I was important—like I was somebody, by-God.

Once again I felt like he was reading my mind when he said, "A. B., you don't need Buddy or anybody else to be important. That's something you must find within yourself. Sooner or later you must start believing in something, so why not start with yourself? You have the capability to do great things in your life, but you must believe in your own possibilities. Even though your parents made some pretty bad choices, they were their choices, not yours. Trust me. You can become who or what you want to be."

You're crazy, old man, I thought to myself. *My pockets are empty and my life stinks!*

He didn't seem to notice that I hadn't responded. He just kept on talking: "Son, I know you're frustrated

18

and I don't blame you. Life hasn't given you much to feel positive about up until now, but that can change. You have a sharp mind, a courageous spirit, and a good heart. You made a good choice not to hang around with Buddy and your other friends tonight, because otherwise you wouldn't be sitting here sharing your beans with me." He chuckled, as if amused by his own joke.

He paused for a moment to pick up a stick and stoke the fire. "Your life is built by the choices you make," he said. "Sometimes things happen that are outside your control and it just doesn't seem right. Life isn't fair, so quit expecting it to be. It's not what happens to you that matters as much as what you choose to do with it. You might choose to feel sorry for yourself and hang around with your pals acting like a tough guy. But playing the role of the victim or the vigilante will both end up leading to a dead-end. That's not where you really want to go. Is it?"

> **"Your life is built by the choices you make."**
> **—The Old Man**

His line of reasoning was beginning to irritate me. *How does this old prospector know so much about me? How does he know what I'm thinking? I don't know myself what I want, so how does he? And where does he get off calling me a victim? I didn't ask for parents who were screwed up— but I'm not asking anybody to feel sorry for me either. Besides, who needs a family anyway? And all that talk about being a vigilant—I don't know the meaning of the word. But I don't need anybody and I'm sure as hell not going to take any lip from this old coot or anybody else. If somebody messes with me they'll get their ass kicked, for sure.*

The old man seemed to sense that I was getting a little heated—and not because of the fire he was stoking in front of us, but the one he had stoked inside of me.

He took a deep breath, sighed audibly, and said, "Son, I'd like to help you. It wasn't an accident that you got born, in spite of the difficulties you have encountered. In fact, those difficulties were no accident either because every problem you have experienced has in some way helped to build your character. In essence, the size of a man's problems determines the size of the man."

At a loss for words, I sat and stared into the fire. No one had ever talked to me like this before. The old man sat there in silence, too, allowing his words to sink in before continuing. "It wasn't an accident that I showed up here tonight either. Someone told me once: 'When the student is ready, the teacher will appear,' and I believe you are more than ready to improve your life. How about it, A. B.? Are you willing to change?"

At this point I was so dazed and confused I could hardly talk. "Well, I guess so," I said, although I was really thinking to myself: *Who is this guy and how can he speak with such authority about life, especially my life?*

The old man stared at me, reading my face more than listening to my words. I could tell he didn't believe me. Finally he said, "If you have enough faith you can move mountains. Have you ever heard that expression?"

"No, I can't say that I have. I don't know much about faith, but I do know about mountains. I've had mountains of trouble since I was a kid."

The old man's face reflected compassion and also wisdom. "Yes, I know, but your luck is changing, kid. Actually faith is only a small part of the whole package—but an important part, no doubt, because faith can ignite the courage to take action. It's similar to the way spark plugs ignite gasoline to run a car. Taking action is your spark plug. Without it you're not going anywhere, so faith alone won't do you much good. You must add action to faith if you want your life to work. In other words, you've got to show up!"

Now I was really confused. "Let me get this

straight," I said. "You're telling me that if I just show up I'll be successful?"

"Yes, that's part of it, but you also have to show up like you mean it. In other words, you can always spot the person with enough faith to move a mountain—he's the guy who shows up with a shovel in his hands and ready to get to work."

The old man took a bite of beans. "Nothing's going to move in your life until you do. You might face mountains of difficulty but not one inch more than you can handle, especially if that handle has the blade of a shovel attached to the end of it."

My head was almost spinning. All this talk about faith and mountains and shovels was mind-boggling. I wasn't used to talking about philosophy, especially when I was with Buddy and my other friends. But my stomach was full and the fire was warm. Suddenly I felt very sleepy.

"Why don't you get some rest?" said the old man. "You have a long day ahead of you, and I also have a great distance to travel and promises to keep. So shut your eyes and go to sleep."

My eyes were already closing by then, and the next thing I remember was awakening to a sky turning red with the morning dawn. There was a shovel in my hand and the old man was gone.

SHOW UP

Mr. Lincoln walked over and picked up the shovel leaning against the wall in the corner of his office. He stood there for a moment gazing at it like it was an old friend he had been reunited with after a long spell. "If I didn't have this shovel for proof, I'd have sworn the encounter I had with the old man that night was all a dream," he said. "But it was real, and to be flat out honest with you, Jason, it was really weird. If I hadn't seen it with my own eyes, I wouldn't have believed it."

A.B. TELLS JASON ABOUT HOW HE
GOT HIS FIRST GOOD JOB USING HIS
NEW SHOVEL

Later that morning I was walking down the sidewalk with the shovel over my shoulder and suddenly I heard a voice say, "Hey you with the shovel!" I looked around to see who the voice belonged to and there was a guy wearing a hardhat standing in front of a construction site. He waved to catch my eye. "Yeah, you kid, come over here."

When I walked over to where he was standing, he asked me if I knew how to use my shovel. "Sure I can," I told him. "I can do anything you need done with this shovel."

I don't know if it was my talk with the old man or what, but at that point I felt confident that I could do anything I set my mind to. Dang, I don't think I've ever felt that way before!

He asked me if I'd like to go to work for him and I jumped at the chance, thinking *Oh, boy. Now I can eat something better than beans.* He hired me right away and put me to work shoveling sand into a concrete mixer. And every day afterward, when I showed up at the construction site, he found me and my shovel something to do. The best part was that he paid me cash at the end of each day.

Showing up with that shovel earned me my first real job. Oh, I had done deliveries and mowed lawns for small change, but this was my first real "grown-up" job. After a few weeks I had saved enough money to find a place to live, and my new apartment over Mrs. Beasley's garage was a lot better than sleeping by the tracks or in abandoned cars.

The apartment was a one-room efficiency with old, beat-up furniture, but it was mine. My life was a whole lot better than when I was hanging out on the street. Mrs. Beasley was a portly woman who always wore a faded gingham dress with an apron. She smelled of cinnamon from her continuous baking. I appreciated the fact that she allowed me to use the washer and dryer in the garage so I could start the day in clean clothes, like the other workers.

A.B. TELLS JASON ABOUT HOW HE MET RALPH, AND WHAT HE TOLD RALPH ABOUT HIS FAMILY HISTORY

Ralph Peters was a construction foreman who took an interest in me. He was very good at giving advice in small chunks so I could chew on them and learn something. He was well over six feet tall and built like a bear. His skin was the color of ebony and he had a soft, deep voice. He always wore a heavy tool belt, and by the size of his forearms you could tell that he was no stranger to repeated heavy lifting and hard work. Ralph had pumped a lot of iron—not in a gym but on construction sites. It wasn't just his size and strength that men respected. He also possessed a strong, silent quality that I admired and wanted for myself.

Ralph showed up every day with a smile on his face and a positive attitude. He was always in a good frame of mind, and I don't remember him ever having a crummy day. At the time I remember thinking: *Man, he sure is a lucky s.o.b.*

The thing I liked most about Ralph was that he was a good listener and he was interested in what I had to say. This included when I spilled my guts about how my mom was always depressed when I was a kid, and how she spent most of the time in her bedroom smoking cigarettes and lying in bed watching television and sleeping. Whenever I went into her room her eyes were always sad and droopy and real dark underneath. If you put a bloodhound in a dress, that's what my mother would have looked like. She rarely said more than a few words before she would tell me to go outside and play until my father came home. Now years later, as I look back on it, I realize she was clinically depressed and in desperate need of help. But at the time I don't think she felt she had any options.

My father worked long hard hours as a laborer at the mill. He always had alcohol on his breath when he came home at night. I suppose he drank to cope with my mother's depression—or maybe it was the other way around: she was depressed because he was always drunk. I don't remember ever seeing them show any affection toward each other. He slept on the couch every night and was gone before I got up in the morning.

One day I came home from school and went to her room to ask if she needed anything. She was lying on the bed with her eyes open but she wasn't moving. I shook her but she didn't respond. There was an empty pill bottle on the nightstand. The police and medical people told us later she had probably died early that morning from a drug overdose. I guess she decided that dying was the only way to find peace.

I didn't know what to think about it and I certainly didn't know how to grieve. As a twelve-year-old boy, all I could think was: *If I had been a better son maybe she would have been happier—and maybe this wouldn't have happened.* But it did happen. She was gone and there was no one to talk to about it. Even if there had been someone, I was so confused I wouldn't have known what to say.

Life got worse after she was gone. My father gradually began to drink more and more. It was probably his way of dealing with his pain. The more he drank the meaner he got. At first he only yelled at me but then things got ugly. He would get drunk and beat the tar out of me with a belt. When I cried he would call me a wimp and lock me in my room. My hatred for him grew, but oddly at the same time I felt sorry for him because he was a sad, pitiful man.

One thing I knew for sure was I that had to get out of there or I was going to die. So when I was sixteen years old I ran away and never looked back. I dropped out of school and started hanging around with Buddy and his gang, as I've mentioned before. Most of them were amateur thieves and small time hoodlums, but they were the only friends I had. At least with them I felt like I belonged somewhere.

After I told Ralph about my past, he said some of the same things the old man had said while we were sitting by the railroad tracks that night: Life is about choices and even though my parents made some pretty bad choices, they were their choices not mine. He told me that I didn't have to continue being a victim of their choices. I could change and become who or what I wanted to be. He also talked about life being unfair and the fact that our past experiences aren't really all that important.

Ralph said that a windshield on a car is a hundred times bigger than the rear view mirror because what's in front of us is a whole lot more important than what is behind. "Kid, you're facing the wrong direction," he said. "Life's unfair sometimes, so you can't use that as an excuse. You've just got to deal with it and move on with your life."

"That's easy for you to say. Your mother didn't commit suicide and your old man wasn't an abusive drunk," I replied.

He had a strange look about him, and I couldn't tell what he was feeling. Was it anger or disappointment? But then his face softened into a sad smile and he seemed to look right through me. "Someday when we have more time I'll tell you a story about...." At the time I thought he said "changing attitude," but later I understood it was something about "change *and* attitude." What a difference a few words can make!

A few weeks later, when we had stopped work to eat lunch, the sky opened up. It was raining so hard the ducks were walking because they couldn't fly underwater. Ralph and I ran to one of the equipment sheds to wait it out. He said there wasn't any use getting soaked twice. When it became apparent that the storm wasn't going to let up, we could hear people starting their vehicles to leave. The sound of the rain beating against the roof and not being able to see past the building in front of us gave us the feeling we were completely isolated. Then lightning knocked out the power and we were sitting there in the dark.

Ralph grabbed his thermos and poured us both a cup of coffee. The fragrant smell of the warm drink began to fill the shed as the cup warmed my hands.

"Kid, we're not going anywhere for a while, so we

have some time on our hands." He sighed and seemed pensive as he stared out at the rain. "Maybe this would be a good time to tell you a story I haven't shared with many people. It's not a real happy story and it's difficult to think about, but it might be worth telling."

I had never heard that tone in his voice before, and my curiosity was definitely aroused. I sat there spellbound listening to Ralph talk about his family.

RALPH TELLS A.B. ABOUT HIS PERSONAL TRAGEDY

I was raised in a family of six kids and I was the oldest. My mom and dad were good people who worked hard to provide for us. We didn't have a lot of material wealth, but our parents tried hard to show us kids how much they loved us. We were a close-knit family and we looked out for each other—especially our youngest brother, Toby, who was special to everyone in the family because he had been born with Down's syndrome. We all loved and cared for that little guy.

Life was good until I was seventeen and then my whole world turned upside down. One night when I was over at the neighbor's place helping build a new fence, two inmates escaped from the prison over in the next county and were running from the law. They just happened to wander up to our farm where they hid out in the barn. When my dad went out to feed the cattle and to do his nightly chores he must have startled them. They killed him with a pitchfork and left him lying in the barn.

That little taste of blood must have made them bolder and thirsty for more. After they killed my dad, they went into the house and found my mom in the kitchen. My brother said he heard the man screaming at her to shut up and be still or he would kill her kids.

After the kids were tied up in the dining room, the other inmate set his eyes on my fourteen-year-old sister, Sarah. He untied her and dragged her by her hair into mom and dad's bedroom. My twelve-year-old brother, Michael, managed to wiggle free from the ropes and help the others get loose. Then he ran about a half mile down the road to the neighbors, where I was helping build the fence. I dropped everything and ran home as fast as I could, only to find my dad lying in the barn with the pitchfork still in his chest. I found my mom in the kitchen lying in a puddle of blood. Probably the most painful thing of all was finding my beautiful, precious little sister, Sarah, lying on the bed. She was dead with her eyes still open.

I couldn't stop thinking over and over again: *If only I'd been there…if only…if only…then none of this would have happened.* I cried and cried, but no amount of tears or guilt was going to bring them back. I hated those men and I hated God, too, for standing by and doing nothing while my family was brutally murdered. It didn't make any sense to me then and it still doesn't. Some things just never make sense.

I became a man that day. I had to. I had two little brothers and two little sisters to take care of, so I left school and worked the family farm so I could raise those kids. The neighbors helped some, but there was no other family to help us. The folks from the state agency looked in on us once or twice a month for about a year, but when the original caseworker quit the new one seemed to lose interest and eventually stopped coming by.

That was over thirty years ago, but I can still remember it like it was yesterday. It was real hard for a couple of years. Those kids began to look at me like a father and I fiercely loved and protected every one of them. Michael grew up to be a fireman. I don't know what he likes more, the feeling he gets from rescuing people who need it or the adrenaline he gets from rushing into dangerous situations and putting out fires.

Lisa, my sister next to Michael, became a nurse at the local hospital because she loves helping people. She got married and had a couple of kids of her own, and she seems happy.

Our other sister, Janie, is a mess. She's been married a couple of times and can't seem to settle down.

Maybe she just never got over losing our parents and sister that way.

As for Toby, he lives with me and my wife Ginny. Our two kids adore him, and he is still as precious and innocent as he was when he was a little boy. What can I say about him other than he is simply happy for no reason, which is not a bad way to be.

A.B. REACTS TO RALPH'S FAMILY TRAGEDY

Ralph finished his story by telling me the two inmates were later killed in a shootout with the state police. They buried his mom and dad, and his sister in the family plot high on a hill under a big oak tree. He said they had a real nice view of the countryside and he imagined they would find peace there.

At that point I felt like pure crap for bellyaching about my problems, and I was glad the lights were still out when he had finished talking. His voice never wavered but I thought I saw tears on his cheeks during the flashes of lightning. One thing was for sure, I could not trust my own voice to speak because I was crying quietly for both of us—his family and my Mom. I had never admitted to myself how much her leaving had hurt me.

Ralph and I passed the time in silence, each with

our own personal grief. Only when it started to get dark was I finally able to speak. "I'm sorry I acted like such a whiner. Your family went through hell, and I don't understand how you ever got over hating those guys for what they did. How can something so horrible happen to good people? It just doesn't make sense. Why is life so unfair?"

"I don't know why these things happen," said Ralph. "And I have to admit I went through years of being bitter over what those two scumbags did to me and my family. I could have held onto that grudge the rest of my life, but I realized that I wasn't hurting anybody but myself and my brothers and sisters. My bitterness caused me to be negative and overly critical—of myself and the people I loved the most.

"Eventually I turned to the bottle to try and kill the pain of those awful memories but that just made it worse. Sometimes you have to hit bottom before you can finally look up. When I finally crashed, thankfully my wife Ginny was there to help pick me up. I got into a twelve-step program, which probably saved my life. No matter how rough your life is, there comes a time when you have to let go of the past. It might not be fair but you can't change your history. Sooner or later you just have to deal with it. My biggest struggle was being angry at God. How could He ignore things like what happened to my family and not do anything about it? I don't understand it. But one thing I've learned from experience is that it doesn't do any good to get mad at God.

> **"No matter how rough your life is, there comes a time when you have to let go of the past. It might not be fair but you can't change your history."—Ralph Peters**

"Yeah, we can't go running to God to bail us out every time something bad happens. Besides, He's probably got better things to do anyway," I said.

Ralph laughed at my comment. "There's a whole lot about God that we will never understand—even if we live to be a hundred and twenty," he said. "Our view is much more limited than His. It's like God sees the whole parade of our lives but we only see one float at a time. God is generous and he gave me the strength to let go and move on with my life.

"I made a choice over twenty years ago to put a smile on my face and show up every day with a good attitude. It's my choice, and since I made that decision it sure has become easier for my family and friends to be around me. Most importantly, it's a lot easier to live in my own skin. It beats the hell out of being grumpy all the time, and people are much nicer to me. Sure, there are still some people who are rude and obnoxious, but just because they act that way is no reason I have to. I'm the person I choose to be—and not because of what others do or don't do.

"So, who do you choose to be, A. B., and how are you going show up each day? I was really impressed when I first met you. Showing up with a shovel in your hand told me you are definitely not afraid of work. Now all you have to do is improve your attitude and remember to smile, kid. It doesn't cost one nickel more to be happy." With that, Ralph grinned and gave me a wink.

A.B. IS GIVEN THE FIRST LAW OF THE SHOVEL

About that time the lights came back on and we sat there blinking for a minute. "I guess that's our sign to get on home," said Ralph, screwing the cup back on his thermos.

Even though we had been sitting there in the shed for most of the afternoon, I was pretty drained, mentally and emotionally. It felt like I had just worked two shifts back to back. My conversation with Ralph had certainly made me look at things differently.

I worked on that particular job for another six months, showing up every day with a positive attitude and a smile on my face. Ralph was right. As I became happier and more confident and sure of myself, people were a lot friendlier to me.

Then one day the project was finished and all the day laborers were dismissed, including me. The construction superintendent pulled me aside and said they were starting a new job across town, and if I wanted more work to show up early the next morning.

That night as I drifted off to sleep, I thought about all that had happened over the past six months, and how my life had changed since that night by the railroad tracks. During the night the old man visited me in a dream—or maybe it was real. Anyway, I vividly remember him saying, "A. B., if you want to move mountains in your life, show up with a shovel—and don't forget to bring along a positive attitude. No one ever erected a monument honoring a pessimist."

The next morning when I picked up my shovel I smelled a familiar burnt smell, like I smelled once after lightning struck a pole near where I was standing. When I looked at the shovel these words were etched into the blade:

I. Show Up

It was the First Law of the Shovel, and I had a pretty good grasp of what it meant and how important it was in my life. As I sat there staring at the shovel and thinking about my mysterious encounter with the old man, I tried to rationalize and analyze everything, but there wasn't a logical explanation. Just like Ralph said, some things just don't make sense, even if you have all the facts.

After I had eaten breakfast I pulled the piece of paper with the address of the next job out of my pocket. I realized that if I was going to make some money that day I had better start walking.

3

HABITS MAKE OR BREAK YOU

I was totally absorbed in Mr. Lincoln's story when his assistant, Ann, entered the office carrying a tray of food from the cafeteria. Man, did it look good—grilled chicken breast, baked beans, glazed carrots, and a bowl of blackberry cobbler. It just doesn't get any better than that. I could get used to this type of treatment, for sure.

"Jason, let's move over to the table and chow down on this good food while I continue my story," said A.B.

We moved over to the huge conference table where Ann had meticulously placed the food and drinks on one end. The view from the window was breathtaking, and I gazed out thinking: *Now this is the life.*

After pouring me a glass of iced tea, Mr. Lincoln

said, "Okay, where was I? Oh yeah, I remember...I showed up outside the gate of that new jobsite with my shovel on my shoulder. It was apparent that there were more men than jobs. My old superintendent, Jim Stevens, was standing inside the gate with a man in a suit, who pointed right at me. Mr. Stevens walked over to the gate and called my name. I was standing near the back of the crowd and received more than a few angry stares from the men, but they parted to let me through. Most of them were a lot older than me and couldn't understand why a young guy like me was going to be the first one hired.

But I was the only one with a shovel on my shoulder. This was the second time I learned the power of showing up with a shovel.

"Son, do you always show up with that shovel?" said the man in the suit.

"Yes, sir, I do."

"That's a great habit, kid. With those kinds of habits you'll have great success in life."

A.B. TELLS JASON ABOUT JEFF HOWELL AND JEFF'S HEALTHY HABITS

Speaking of habits, Jason—I learned some valuable lessons about habits while working at that jobsite. I met a brick mason there named Jeff Howell, who became instrumental in changing my life—in ways I never expected. Jeff sort of reminded me of Ralph because he came to work every day with a smile on his face and a cheerful attitude. His diet was also quite impressive. It might sound a little strange, but food was one of his strategies for winning.

Jeff told me, "You are what you eat," and from the looks of his physique I had to agree. He was a *specimen*, alright! He was rippled with muscles and didn't have an ounce of fat on him. He called himself a "triathlete," although at the time I didn't have the foggiest idea what that meant. Turns out he competed in these races called "triathlons," which are a combination of swimming, bicycling, and running. He said triathlons required strength and endurance, the same as life. From what the guys around the construction site said about him, Jeff was a pretty good athlete. At the time, he was training for a new kind of race that was being formulated in Hawaii. They called it the "Ironman," and the organizers claimed it would be the "mother" of all races. It took about eight hours to complete. I didn't know anything about it at the time, but Jeff sure looked like an Ironman to me.

As I said, he was very meticulous about the way he ate. He brought his lunch to work every day—I say lunch, but really he ate five or six times a day. He called it "grazing." According to Jeff, it's better to eat several small meals during the day rather than one or two big ones—unlike the way I ate, which was usually about once a day. I would skip breakfast and maybe have a Twinkie or something sweet to snack on at lunch, and then go home and have a TV dinner or take-out hamburgers and fries washed down with a Coke.

Jeff ate celery with peanut butter and carrots in the mid-morning and afternoon. At lunch he had tuna or turkey, with fruit and cottage cheese. Talk about being a fanatic! The guy didn't have a weight problem, but he firmly believed that a low-fat, high-carbohydrate diet gave him an extra edge. So, even though he burned almost 5,000 calories a day from exercising and working at the job, he would literally rinse his cottage cheese to get the extra fat off. Talk about self-discipline! He practiced good eating habits and anything else he thought might improve his performance—whether it was winning a race or something else he wanted to achieve.

I can just imagine Jeff running a 26-mile marathon in hundred-degree heat on the black, baked volcanic lava beds of the Hawaiian coast after swimming a grueling 2.4 wave-tossed miles in the ocean, and then bicycling 112 miles against ferocious crosswinds –while thinking to himself: *Hey, after rinsing my cottage cheese every day this ain't half bad!*

There must have been something to his eating thing, because I swear that guy could outwork four men. He made such an impression on me that I went to the grocery store one day after work and bought a lunchbox, so I could start packing food every day just like him. I would cut up some carrots and celery, and pack a can of tuna or turkey with a few pieces of fruit and a bag of mixed nuts. I just couldn't do the cottage cheese thing, though. It looked too much like baby vomit to me. We began to eat lunch together every day, and Jeff even convinced me to start eating breakfast, too. After only a few weeks, I felt stronger; my thinking was sharper; and I had a lot more energy.

One day while we were eating lunch, Jeff said, "A.B., I have an extra bicycle you can use if you'd like to start riding with me some in the evenings. And by the way, you really need to put down those cigarettes. That habit can kill you."

Of course he was right. I had started smoking to look tough, and to tell you the truth I didn't even like it at first. But after awhile smoking became automatic. It was one of the first things I reached for in the morning and the last thing I did before going to bed. I knew cigarettes were bad for me because I was beginning to cough every morning. That's the way bad habits are— first you pick them up and then they put you down.

Jeff kept after me until I finally agreed to go bike

riding with him. I really enjoyed our long rides on the back country roads, smelling fresh cut alfalfa hay and feeling the cool breeze on my face. We had some long talks and became good friends. I liked riding so much that I bought my own bicycle, and the next thing you know, he had me running and swimming, too. Jeff said he was going to turn me into a triathlete.

By the way, after I got into the habit of exercising I gave up smoking, because a person just can't do both. Jeff said this one of the great secrets about healthy habits—if you want to give up a bad habit, cultivate a good one to replace it. It sure worked for me. I've been smoke-free ever since.

> **"If you want to give up a bad habit, cultivate a good one to replace it."**
> **—Jeff Howell**

Everybody has habits, Jason, but the ones you choose will either make you or break you. Your future depends on the habits you choose to develop today. The key to developing good habits is consistence and persistence. Being consistent means doing things the same way, over and over. For example, when we find the right amounts of cement, sand, and water we can combine them and make great concrete. The habit of using the same formula over and over again gives us consistent quality.

The habit of being persistent means we keep trying. Things don't always work out the way we planned because of forces beyond our control. For example, bad weather can ruin a framework we set up and we'll have to tear it down and start over. Once we even had a tornado demolish a building that was almost completed, but we cleared away the rubble and started over again. Sometimes these things happen in other areas of our lives, too. Success comes because of our persistence in getting up and trying again.

Jeff also taught me the importance of hanging around with people who could help me grow in a positive direction. He said that it's hard to soar like an eagle if you're hanging around with a bunch of turkeys. He told me that each person becomes an "average" of the five people they hang around with the most because the attitudes and habits of others rub off on us. Essentially, we are the company we keep.

He asked if I'd like to go with him to his regular Friday night meeting and get to know some folks who might have a positive influence on me. He had already convinced me to try and spruce up my social life so I agreed. But he didn't tell me until we got there that it was a Bible study group. He probably knew that if he had told me ahead of time, I wouldn't go—and he was probably right. At the time I didn't have any use for religion or hanging around with a bunch of Jesus freaks.

But these folks were different. They didn't try to cram religion down my throat. There wasn't any of that "Thee" or "Thou" crap that I had heard from those stuff-shirted preachers who were just trying to get their hands into my wallet. They talked about real issues. They also seemed to be having a lot of fun, which was another thing I wasn't used to. Anyway, it was impressive. They had a lot of *something* the guys I'd been hanging around with didn't have—a kind of personal contentment and happiness. And to tell you the truth, there were a couple of girls in the group who were really cute and friendly. This definitely made me want to go back, so eventually I developed another positive habit. If you had told me before that I would start going to a Bible study group, I would have said you were one brick short of a load. But I liked Jeff's group and started going regularly.

Jeff also helped me to get a good deal on my first truck, a blue 1962 Ford pick-up. It was used and battered but beautiful to me. Man, was I ever proud of that truck. You would have thought it was a Ferrari. He also taught me about the habit of saving money. He explained the power of compound interest and that if I put a certain percentage of my paycheck in a savings account, over time it would turn into a pretty big nest egg. He said eventually I would start earning enough interest so that my money would start working for me instead of me working for my money.

I began saving twenty percent of every penny I made, and you wouldn't believe how much that habit has produced over the years with compound interest. It's kind of confusing, but "compound" interest is money you earn on interest you have already earned! All that interest, plus some of the other investments I've made, has generated enough passive income to cover my living expenses and much more. (By "passive income" I mean I didn't have to do anything to make it happen!) In other words, I don't *have* to work anymore. My job is still enjoyable, but it's no longer a rat race. And let me tell you something, Jason. It doesn't matter if you win that race—a rat is still a rat.

Those were some of the best days of my life. Jeff taught me a whole lot about eating healthy food, exercising regularly, and competing in triathlons. These habits inspired me to install the cafeteria and exercise facilities in our building here, so our associates can take care of themselves and develop healthy habits, too.

We also have various book study and personal accountability groups that meet conveniently here on our campus to help people grow personally and professionally. In addition, we have a savings plan for all of our associates. If you commit to saving ten percent of your income in a long-term account, we'll match it dollar for dollar. We want you to be successful and get out of the rat race, too.

Jeff introduced me to another wonderful thing. She was five-foot-seven, with strawberry-blond hair and the most beautiful, piercing green eyes I've ever seen. Her name was Juliann Parker, and I can sum up what I thought about her in two words: Hubba! Hubba! She was in our Friday night Bible study group, and boy did she ever come into my life like a firestorm. I'll tell you more about her later.

A.B. IS GIVEN THE SECOND LAW OF THE SHOVEL

Two years had passed since my first encounter by the railroad tracks with the old man, but then he showed up again. I was driving to work one day and noticed him standing in a large, well-tended garden at the end of a row in bib overalls. He was smiling at me and leaning on his shovel. I parked by the edge of the garden and as I was walking toward him, he said, "A. B., look at my garden and tell me what you see."

I turned and saw a row of luscious tomatoes, my favorite vegetable. There also were rows of squash, peas, and beans. "Those are some great looking tomatoes," I told him. "I like tomatoes a lot and obviously you do, too."

"What kind of seeds do you think produced these tomatoes?" the old man asked.

"I know they didn't come from squash seeds," I said, thinking this might be a trick question.

"That's right, A. B. What you plant determines what you get—and how *much* you get depends on how often you cultivate and water your garden."

He reached down and pulled a weed. "Who do you suppose planted this weed?"

"Nobody plants weeds; they just show up."

"You're right," he said. "Bad habits are like weeds. They just show up and grow without being planted. Eventually they can ruin your garden. Beware of the weeds in your life and get in the habit of pulling them."

> **"Bad habits are like weeds. They just show up and grow without being planted. Eventually they can ruin your garden. Beware of the weeds in your life and get in the habit of pulling them."**
> **—The Old Man**

The next morning when I woke up, I smelled that same familiar burnt smell, like lightning had struck again. I thought to myself: *Hmmm. I think I'm starting to see a pattern here.*

Sure enough, I looked over at my shovel leaning against the wall and saw the new words etched into the blade. It was the Second Law of the Shovel.

II. Habits Make or Break You

I was learning the construction business pretty good about that time and moving up the "ladder of success" through different job assignments. In fact, they put me on full time. I was gaining more and more confidence.

Mr. Stevens, the construction superintendent, came to me one day and said, "A.B. I'd like to send you over to Raleigh for a class to become certified in evaluating steel framing systems for specific project requirements for high floor-to-floor heights and vibration variances. Is that something you'd be interested in?

I didn't really know what he was talking about, but I jumped on it like a duck on a june bug. "Why yes, sir! That's exactly what I've been thinking. That's just how I can put my skills to good use."

He chuckled at my obvious line of bull manure and said, "Good, you'll leave Monday morning for Raleigh. We'll have a van here at the jobsite to pick up you and a couple of other guys. We'll also arrange for hotel rooms and food expenses while you're there. The van will leave at 7:00 a.m. sharp, so be here early. If you do well in the class I'm going to promote you to site inspector and give you a raise. This is a great opportunity, son."

I was on cloud nine the rest of the week. Man, I strutted around that construction site like a little banty rooster. I was going to get a raise and *be somebody*.

Own Your Actions

By this point in the conversation we had finished our lunch and Mr. Lincoln's assistant had cleared the table and brought in some coffee. "Please hold my calls for the rest of the afternoon, Ann," said Mr. Lincoln. "Jason and I are in the middle of an important discussion and I don't want to be disturbed."

Wow. I was blown away! The president of the company considered me important enough to hold his calls—and on my first day with the company. This couldn't be happening. It seemed too good to be true.

"Mr. Lincoln, I don't know what to say. I'm just a rookie architect and yet you're treating me like I'm somebody special. It's only my first day but I'm already your loyal fan—I mean employee."

A.B. laughed. "Jason, there's no such thing as a "rookie" in our company. Every associate is equally valuable, and I'm here to help you do your best. I learned a long time ago that rank has responsibility, not privilege. I don't put myself above anyone in this organization. I learned the hard way that pride just sets you up for painful humiliation."

"It sounds like you're a great student of life, Mr. Lincoln—even though the lessons didn't always come easy."

A.B. TELLS JASON HOW HE LEARNED ABOUT PRIDE

You're right, Jason. I've learned that some of the best gifts don't come nicely wrapped. Getting back to our story, you'll see what I mean. After Mr. Stevens told me about the training in Raleigh, I strutted around the construction site all week acting like my "you-know-what" didn't stink. That Friday night at the Bible study I told Juliann all about my big promotion—actually "gloated" would be a better description. I talked about how important they thought I was at the construction site, and how one of these days I'd be running the show. She listened quietly as I went on and on. When I finished, she stared at me with those piercing green eyes and said simply, "Pride cometh before a fall."

I wasn't quite sure what she meant but I figured

it must be something biblical. I expected her to be impressed, but boy was I ever wrong. She acted like she couldn't care less that I was the "stud duck on the block" at work now. Quite frankly, this woman was starting to irritate me a bit. Actually, in hindsight, that's a huge understatement, but I'll tell you more about that later, too.

Come Monday morning I could hardly contain my excitement as I fixed myself some breakfast and packed my food for the day in my lunchbox. I had never been on a trip like this before and I didn't even own a suitcase, so I packed a black, plastic garbage bag with several changes of clothes and headed for the jobsite to meet the van. I was running a little late but I thought: *No problem. They'll wait for me.*

When I got to the jobsite about 7:20 a.m. there was no van in sight. At first I thought the driver must be running a little late, too. But then I got to thinking it was funny that the other two guys hadn't shown up yet either. I continued to wait, but the longer I waited, the more nervous I became. By about 7:45 I realized they must have left without me. *How could they do that? I was only 20 minutes late. Surely they wouldn't leave without ME.*

I was sitting in front of the jobsite when Mr. Stevens drove up a little after 8:00. He looked at me and said, "You were late. The driver called me about fifteen after seven and I told him to leave without you. Go back to your old job and let that be a lesson to you, kid. When you get an opportunity in the future, make sure you *show up on time*."

He turned and walked into his office. I was so upset I didn't think my legs would hold me up. At first I was numb. I didn't know what to think. I was only twenty minutes late. Surely they wouldn't punish me for being a little late. This couldn't be happening.

I walked across the jobsite to my workstation in a state of humiliation. I had been bragging to the guys for a week about my upcoming training and big promotion. How could I face them? Humble pie is sure hard to swallow with your pride…and a lot of good that pride was doing me now. Oh how I regretted being so cocky.

The more I thought about it, the angrier I became. I had worked hard and I deserved that promotion. Bad news travels fast, and in no time at all everybody at the jobsite knew about my screw-up. Guys were snickering and joking about it behind my back, but I could still hear them. My temper got pretty short and I even threatened to whip one guy's butt because he called me "inspector."

It was definitely a lousy week. My attitude went south and I lost my smile. Some old thoughts and feelings began to surface: *You can't trust anybody…Success isn't for the likes of me…Get the other guy before he gets you…Nobody else cares so why should I?*

I even entertained thoughts of looking up Buddy and the old gang. Maybe they would respect me more than the guys on the job. Interestingly, the real issue wasn't that people began to disrespect me, but rather that I had lost respect for myself. I had messed up, and now I needed to admit it. Instead of blaming others for my circumstances, I needed to own up to my actions.

It's easy to blame other people for the events that happen in our lives. This is behavior we all fall into pretty easily. But I found, rather painfully, that one of the most important keys to growth—and success—is the fact that we cannot change the things we don't own.

> **"Instead of blaming others for my circumstances, I needed to own up to my actions. We cannot change the things we don't own."**
> **—A.B. Lincoln**

I should have been on time. I missed an opportunity because of my own actions, not the actions of the van driver, Mr. Stevens, or the guys on the job. I needed to take ownership of the fact that I was responsible for creating my circumstances, although it took me a couple of weeks to figure it out. Yeah, I continued to show up at work every day, but with a bad attitude and a chip on my shoulder. I was wound up tighter than an eight-day clock and didn't have a friend in the world to talk to about it. It's interesting how anger and blame create a wall of isolation between us and the world.

A.B. TALKS ABOUT HOW JULIANN AND THE OLD MAN TAUGHT HIM TO CHANGE HIS ATTITUDE

At this point Mr. Lincoln poured himself another cup of coffee, walked over to the window, and gazed out at the city below. He seemed deep in thought for a moment, reflecting on his memories. Then he came back to his chair and said, "You know, Jason, we get exactly what we need in life just at the right time—whether we realize it or not. A couple of weeks later I ran into Juliann Parker at the grocery store. She was real friendly and seemed glad to see me, but I was embarrassed after doing all that bragging about my promotion.

"We've missed you at the Bible study group the last couple of weeks," she said. "I'm sorry to hear about what happened with your job. Jeff Howell told me it fell through."

There was no way I was going to let her know how disappointed I was, so I put up a tough guy front. "No skin off my nose," I said. "It's their loss. Anyway, I'm just doing this job until my uncle gets me a truck driver's job over in Charlotte, which should be any time." It was a lie. I didn't even have an uncle in Charlotte, but I couldn't let my feelings show.

Of course Juliann didn't believe me. "Well before you go to Charlotte to be a truck driver or run off and join the French Foreign Legion or something else dramatic, I'd really like to talk to you more about this, A.B. When was the last time you had a home-cooked meal?"

"Hmmm, home-cooked meal…home-cooked meal. Do you mean people really cook meals at home?" I said, trying to lighten up the conversation a little.

She laughed. "Yeah, some people cook. Why don't you come to my house and I'll fix you a real home-cooked meal. *And* I promise to make it low-fat. Jeff Howell told me that you have become as fanatical as he is about eating healthy. How about this Thursday?"

"I'll have to check my calendar. Well what do you know; I just had a cancellation so I guess I'm free on Thursday," I said, making a joke.

"Great!" she said, giving me a mischievous grin. "I'll see you at 7:00 p.m. and *don't be late.*"

"Oh, I won't be," I said, trying to hide my embarrassment. Whether she intended to or not, her comment had struck a deep chord in me. Having blown the last 7:00 opportunity, there was no way I would let it happen again.

The next couple of days went a little better at

work. At least I wasn't mad enough to whip somebody's butt, even though I still felt like a knife was stuck in my gut. I kept to myself and didn't say a lot, except to Jeff when we ate lunch. I told him about my dinner date with Juliann, and he said he had known her for a long time and that she was one of the finest people he had ever met. "She's cute and incredibly smart, too," he said. "She might not waste air with too many words but when she does talk, you can bet that what she says is worth taking seriously."

Thursday evening came and I arrived at her house early, five minutes before seven. She met me at the door, and I swear I've never been in the presence of anyone so beautiful. Her long hair was pulled back to expose her neck, which looked as soft as silk, and she smelled as pretty as she looked. For a moment, all I could do was stand there with my mouth gaped open.

She offered me a glass of iced tea and showed me around her house. Everything was very neat and uncluttered. It was apparent that she lived simply yet tastefully. She didn't have a lot of furniture but what she had was nice. I liked it immediately and thought: *This is the way I'm going to live someday.*

She took me through the kitchen and out to the deck in the backyard. The table was already set and the food smelled delicious. I couldn't remember the last time I had eaten a home-cooked meal. I usually ate a handful of sliced turkey or woofed down a can of tuna with some carrots and broccoli while standing at my kitchen sink—before getting ready to go for a bike ride, a run, or a swim. So this was a real treat.

Baked turkey breast, fresh cranberry sauce, baked sweet potatoes, asparagus, and sliced cucumbers—I've never forgotten Juliann's home-cooked meal. Even though it was early October, it sure seemed like Thanksgiving—especially when she said there was homemade pumpkin pie for dessert.

While we ate dinner I asked her to tell me more about herself and her life growing up. She had a younger brother; her dad was a carpenter; and her mom was a school teacher. Both of her parents loved to read and had a strong spiritual faith, but they weren't overly religious. She said her dad was a very generous man with a great sense of humor, and although he didn't attend church much, he was the best Christian she had ever met. She said her dad definitely believed in "walking the walk, instead of just talking the talk." Juliann was a whole lot like her daddy.

She told me she was a student at the local community college, majoring in business, and she worked part-time in the Admissions Office. She also sold health and skin care products part-time for Mary Kay Cosmetics, which must have been why she had such a glow to her skin. She poured me a second glass of tea and said, "So tell me how you're doing, A.B. You're not really going to drive trucks in Charlotte are you?"

"No, I'm not going to drive trucks." At that point I didn't have the nerve tell her I didn't really have an uncle in Charlotte, although I suspect she already knew. So I simply tried to skim over the subject by saying, "It's been a tough couple of weeks. As you know, I was up for a promotion and kind of got the shaft on that deal. But that's okay. I'll eventually find a job where they appreciate my hard work."

She asked me to tell her more about what happened so I gave her the grim details—from my point of view, of course. She listened without saying a word other than occasionally saying something like, "And how do you feel about that?"

I talked for a long while and finally got everything off my chest. She sat there in silence for a moment after I had stopped talking and then she said, "A.B. It's not what happens to you that matters as much as what you choose to do with it."

"You haven't been talking to an old guy with a donkey and a shovel down by the railroad tracks have you?" I responded.

"An old man…where?"

"Oh, nothing. It just seems like I've heard those words before. So tell me, what do you think about what happened?"

Juliann had a lot to say. "First of all—and I don't mean to be critical—but maybe it's time to own the consequences of your actions. You agreed to show up on time and Mr. Stevens made a promise to you based on this requirement. When you didn't keep your end of the agreement, things fell apart. You didn't like it, and I bet Mr. Stevens didn't either. You were both counting on a certain outcome but it didn't happen the way you expected. Now you have some choices. You can blame your boss or your co-workers, or you can beat yourself up over it. From listening to you talk, it sounds like you've done some of both, but now it's time to stop the "blame game." Simply own your actions and the results of those actions. When you do this, you'll begin to take control of your life. A.B., have you considered apologizing to Mr. Stevens for letting him down and asking him what you can do to earn his trust again?"

> **"It's time to own the consequences of your actions and stop the 'blame game.'"**
> **—Juliann Parker**

"Do you think it would do any good?"

"It sure couldn't hurt," she said. "I think he sees something in you that you might not see in yourself.

By the way, do you know how diamonds are made?"

"No, not really, but I read someplace once that they come from mines in South Africa and they are a woman's best friend."

She seemed amused by my sense of humor and laughed loudly. "Diamonds begin as a chunk of coal that is placed under an intense amount of heat and pressure. Eventually something extremely valuable is created from the coal, which was once crude and un-polished. I see a diamond in you, A.B., and I believe others do, too. The important thing is for you to em-brace your own possibilities. When you believe in your-self you can't help but be successful!"

"Are you sure you don't know an old man with a donkey and a shovel who hangs around down at the railroad tracks?"

"Who is this old man you keep talking about?" she asked, a confused look on her face.

"Oh, I'll explain it someday. So you think I should go to Mr. Stevens and apologize?"

"Absolutely! If you'll show him that you're willing to own your actions and make things right, I believe he will respect you for it. And it might not be a bad idea to make a few amends with your co-workers, too."

"And how do you suggest I do it?" I asked.

"You can start by lightening up a little. I know you're as tough as nails, but life is much too serious to take yourself so seriously, Mr. Lincoln." She gave me a girlish grin. "And speaking of which, how about a little pumpkin pie?"

We enjoyed some pie and coffee, and spent the rest of the evening not being serious. I must say, it was the best night of my life up to that point. She was the most special human being I had ever met.

When I got ready to leave, she hugged me like I had never been hugged before. Not that I had a lot of experience in that department. In fact, the last time I could remember anyone hugging me was my mother when I was about nine or ten years old. The thing that made Juliann's hug so special was that she wasn't in any hurry to stop. When I told her how much I liked the way she smelled, she put her head against my chest and said, "A.B. Lincoln, you're an incredible man and I believe in you."

I could have stood on her porch soaking up that kind of attention for a long time.

I told her I would see her the next night and report how my conversation went with Mr. Stevens. She gave me a soft kiss on the cheek and thanked me for being in her life.

I believe in you? Thank you for being in my life? Good Lord! Nobody had ever talked to me like that. I didn't really need a car to get home. I could have floated the whole way. I didn't know what I'd done to deserve it, but somebody "upstairs" must have been look-ing out for me!

THE OLD MAN SHOWS UP UNEXPECTEDLY, AND A.B. IS GIVEN THE THIRD LAW OF THE SHOVEL

Speaking of somebody upstairs, the old man had not paid me a visit in some time and I was begin-ning to wonder what had happened to him. The next day while I was walking near a downtown project, I stopped to gaze up at a magnificent, towering office building. I sensed there was someone standing next to me. I looked to my right and there stood the old man. He was quite clean, sporting a neatly trimmed beard, and dressed in an expensive Italian suit. He had every appearance of a highly successful business man, not a dirty old prospector from the railroad tracks.

"Wow, you clean up pretty good," I told him. "Where have you been?"

"Well, you clean up pretty good yourself, my young friend." The old man laughed at his own joke, adding, "I'm always around but you don't see me be-cause you're not looking in the right direction."

Before I could ask what that meant, he contin-ued, "So you like my concrete creation here? Let's go inside and I'll give you a tour. There are some people I want you to meet."

He led me into an elevator and punched the button to the top floor. When we exited the elevator, a smart-looking, young woman with a beautiful smile approached and said, "Sir, they are about to begin in the main conference room." Then she winked at me and said, "Good morning, A.B."

Before I could ask how she knew my name, she turned and left. The old man took me by the arm and escorted me down the hall to a large meeting room. We entered quietly and he pulled out a chair for me at the far end of the table. With his finger on his lips, he signaled to me to be quiet and listen.

At the other end of the table sat a small man wearing a gray suit, white shirt, and a striped tie. His carefully coiffed white hair was combed straight back. He seemed intense to the point of being almost anxious, yet he was self-assured and obviously used to being in charge. The old man told me his name was "Mr. B."

Mr. B. smiled and nodded at me, and then turned to the four men seated two on each side of the table. "Well, gentlemen, you have been managing my money for some time now and it's time for an accounting of what you've accomplished." He briefly scanned a file in front of him, "Fred, I believe you started with ten million; what's my account worth today?"

Fred shuffled through the papers in front of him

and looked up at Mr. B. "Your investments in various negotiable instruments and equities have accrued nicely under my supervision, and you now have twenty million in liquid assets, after all fees and deductions."

"Well done, Fred. That's outstanding."

"Thank you, Mr. B.," Fred said, beaming.

Mr. B. then focused on the man to Fred's left. "Bob, I believe my beginning portfolio with you contained five million. What does it amount to now?"

"Sir, I bought and sold hard assets in real estate and certain financial instruments called "zero coupon bonds" as well as both municipal and corporate bonds. Although I admit my initial reluctance, I did as you instructed and liquidated all of those holdings, so today your account contains ten million dollars in U.S. currency."

"I understand your reluctance, Bob," said Mr. B. "And I know real estate values seemed to be rising astronomically, but we have to take into account that everything in this world runs in cycles. Our accounting process must not just be about the numbers in front of us, but the reality of cycles and bubbles in the market. Greed and stubbornness can sometimes cause people to hold on too long. That's why accountability is so important. You are doing a good job with my assets, and I appreciate your hard work, dedication to detail, and commitment to excellence."

Mr. B. turned to the other side of the table and spoke to the third man, "Luther, you started with one million dollars of my money. So where do we stand today? I believe you have a presentation you wanted to make?"

"Yes, sir," Luther said, a slight tremor in his voice. "First of all I would like to report that I spent a lot of time with the research department and marketing staff, and in my opinion most of them need to be fired for incompetence. I analyzed the "price to earnings ratio" of most stocks on the market, and I believe the market itself has been highly overvalued.

I also believe there is a tsunami of disaster awaiting the real estate market because young people are still leaving the farms headed for the bright lights of the big city, reducing demand for farms and destabilizing farm prices. With the war in Vietnam winding down, the military-industrial complex will lose the power to generate a significant portion of our gross domestic product, and the number of soldiers returning home from the Pacific Rim will destabilize the labor market.

With all the risk in the world today, I didn't want to lose one dime of your money. And knowing how particular you are, I didn't want to lose my job by making a mistake. So I put your money in a safe in my office. I am happy to report that your one million is still there."

Luther let out a big sigh, and I could see the perspiration starting to form on his forehead. It was so quiet in the room you could hear the clock ticking. After a few minutes of staring at Luther, Mr. B. had a lot to say:

"First of all, instead of owning up to your own fears and failures, you accused others. Blaming someone else for your mistakes is the coward's way out, and as if that wasn't bad enough, you tried to make me the bad guy, even though I gave you a million-dollar opportunity in the first place. To take such a gift and stick it in a safe while drawing a salary every day for doing absolutely nothing is what I call *stealing*. And you are FIRED!"

Mr. B. turned to the fourth man seated at the table. "Gabriel, after you take Luther to his office and retrieve my money from the safe please escort him out to the street!"

Mr. B.'s last words to Luther were, "You're damned lucky I'm letting Gabriel escort you out of the building using the elevator instead of throwing you out the window myself!"

The old man touched my arm and we exited quietly. Carefully contemplating the incident I had just witnessed, I didn't say a word.

"A picture is worth ten thousand words," the old man said. "And now you have a good picture of the importance of owning your actions in order to own your life. If you don't own your life, someone else will."

> **"If you don't own your life, someone else will."—The Old Man**

A car horn honked in the street beside me and I turned my head briefly towards the sound. When I turned back the old man was gone.

I went straight to the shovel when I got home. I expected there would be another law etched into it. I had an idea what it might say but I wanted to make sure. I was right. These words had been added to the growing list on the blade:

III. Own Your Actions

Pain can be a great teacher, Jason. I was resolved not to act cocky and start running my mouth off again. Things were really falling into place and my life was starting to make sense. I was taking my licks but I was learning—and Juliann was a large part of it. Somehow I had the feeling that I was no longer alone.

The next morning I was nervous while getting

ready for work. I had some owning-up to do. As I drove to the jobsite I was praying that Mr. Stevens and the other workers would take what I had to say in a positive way.

5

VISUALIZE YOUR FUTURE

At this point in his story Mr. Lincoln got up from his chair and walked over to the window. He looked out for a moment and then turned and said, "Jason, it's too pretty to be inside. Let's go over to the city park and I'll continue my story as we walk.

"You're the boss. If you want to pay me for walking in the park, that's okay."

"It's a normal occurrence here at Lincoln Construction. In fact, we encourage all of our associates to schedule an hour every day (during work hours) to engage in personal development activities, such as exercising in the gym, walking in the park, participating in a yoga class, or meeting with a book study or accountability group. We want all of our associates to be healthy in body, mind, and spirit. Since we started this practice, absenteeism has been reduced drastically; productivity has increased by almost fifty percent; and our employee turnover rate is almost zero," Mr. Lincoln said, smiling. "Not a bad investment, I'd say."

Once again I realized how fortunate I was in finding such a great place to work.

We left the office and walked to the park, which had picnic tables scattered throughout and playground equipment for children. It was encircled by a walking trail, and beautifully landscaped with flowers and shrubs. Incidentally, I later found out that it was named "Lincoln Park" because it was built with money donated by "you-know-who."

A.B. TELLS JASON ABOUT HOW HE STRAIGHTENED THINGS OUT WITH MR. STEVENS AND HIS CO-WORKERS

Okay where did I leave off? Oh yeah, I was going to talk with Mr. Stevens to clear things up. One thing I had already learned was the importance of being on time, so I arrived at his office before eight o'clock that morning. In fact I was also beginning to understand the value of good time management, which means putting "first things first." Crises often occur because people waste time on trivial matters instead of doing what is most critical. Sooner or later, everyone must learn how to decide what is most valuable.

> **"Good time management means 'putting first things first.' Crises often occur because people waste time on trivial matters instead of doing what is most critical."**
> **—A.B. Lincoln**

When Mr. Stevens arrived a few minutes later, I asked him if he would talk with me for a few minutes. He agreed, so I took a deep breath and began. "First of all, I want to apologize for being late to meet the van a couple of weeks ago. You gave me an opportunity for advancement and I made a commitment to show up on time, but I was late. I take full responsibility and I'm very sorry, sir. There is absolutely no excuse for my actions. I am willing to do whatever it takes to make it right and earn back your trust. And I assure you that if you ever give me another opportunity, I won't let you down."

Mr. Stevens was very cordial. "I appreciate your owning up to your actions, A.B. It takes a big man to tell the truth. This shows me that you have the potential for becoming a great leader. Certainly there will be more opportunities here for you in the future."

Then he asked me what I saw myself doing in the future and I told him I hadn't really thought much about it—other than doing the best I could.

"You need to be a little more specific," he said. "Decide what is really important to you. Don't be like most people who aim at nothing in life, and then hit their nonexistent goal with amazing accuracy. Start planning and visualizing your future, because that's where you'll be spending most of your time! Once you get clear about where you're headed in life, the rest is easy."

Mr. Stevens said he was willing to coach me on how to create a clear vision of my future and then make it happen. "Tell you what I'll do, kid," he said. "I'll meet you here at my office at 7:15 every Monday morning and spend a half hour with you working on your future. We'll both have to get up a little earlier but I think it will be worth it. What do you say, A.B.? Are you willing to try?'

He didn't have to ask me twice. I replied immediately, "Yes, sir. I'm willing to do whatever it takes to advance. I really appreciate you offering to take the time to work with me and let me learn from your experience.

"Okay, we have a deal," said Mr. Stevens. "I'll meet you here every Monday morning. And by the way, did I mention there will be homework? We'll begin with your career plans. Your first assignment is to write down what you want to be doing in ten years, and why you want to be doing it. Be specific; don't play small; and don't worry about what it costs. We'll discuss that when we talk about finances. Now get to work, kid. I'll see you on Monday."

It was hard to believe that Mr. Stevens—the most successful person I knew at the time—was offering to coach me. Now I needed to think about the homework. He told me not to play small. What if I told him I wanted his job? Better yet, what if I told him I wanted to own my own construction company in ten years? I kept telling myself: *Calm down and don't get cocky. And remember to be humble.* As I walked to my workstation I made a few stops and apologized to some of the other workers for being a butthead the past couple of weeks.

JULIANN TELLS A.B. ABOUT HOW SHE ACTIVELY CREATES SUCCESS

That night I talked to Juliann and told her the good news about Mr. Stevens offering to coach me. She certainly had something to say about my homework assignment.

"It shouldn't be a problem for you, Mr. Lincoln," she said, as she giggled and poked me in the ribs. "So what *do* you want to be doing ten years from now?"

"In ten years I will own my own construction company," I said boldly.

77

"Then you will—if that's your vision. Now all you have to do is come up with a plan, and it sounds like Mr. Stevens can help you. From what I understand a vision is made up of a series of small steps that enable a person to achieve a goal. As you know I'm an independent consultant for a network marketing company, Mary Kay Cosmetics. When we recruit enough people into our individual businesses—thereby reaching a certain level of sales—Mary Kay Cosmetics gives us money to purchase a new car. Furthermore, the people we recruit indirectly pay us a portion of the money *they* earn. In this way we begin to earn passive income and eventually we become financially independent."

> **"A vision is made up of a series of small steps that enable a person to achieve a goal."**
> **—Juliann Parker**

"So here's my career and financial vision," she continued. "I intend to earn my new car this year and reach financial independence in five years. My daily goal to accomplish this is to make two new contacts a day. This adds up to ten contacts per week, forty per month. This amounts to about ten hours a week, but it adds up even more as I continue to follow my plan over time. Persistence is the key. I have been working this plan for six months, and I firmly believe that in six more months I'll be able to let go of that twenty-year-old clunker I'm driving now and get my new car. Plus I'll generate enough income to quit my part-time job at the college and spend even more time recruiting new people. I plan to continue working toward this goal for the next five years—by which time, Mr. Lincoln, I will be out of the rat race."

"Well alright then," I said. "That sounds like a great vision and a smart plan to get it done." Juliann's motto for success seemed to be "Plan your work and work your plan." This vision stuff was beginning to make a lot of sense.

MR. STEVENS COACHES A.B. ON CREATING A POWERFUL FUTURE

When Monday morning rolled around I showed up at Mr. Stevens' office at 7:00, and I was sitting on the steps waiting for him when he drove up. We went into his office and he fixed us both a cup of coffee. Pulling a spiral notebook out of his filing cabinet and an ink pen from his desk drawer, he slid them across the table to me, saying, "These will be your tools for our coaching sessions. Show up with them each week, just like you've been showing up with your shovel." He smiled and added, "So tell me what you want to be doing ten years from now in your career."

"Well, sir, I've thought about it a lot—and you did say not to play small." I took a big gulp of air and continued answering his question. "I want to own my own construction company in ten years."

This really made Mr. Stevens laugh. "For some reason, I knew you would choose a very big goal, and that's what I like about you, son. So tell me why you made this particular choice."

"I've thought about it quite a bit, sir, and there are actually a couple of reasons. First of all, up until I met you I didn't think much of myself or life in general. My parents certainly didn't give me any hope. I want to amount to something, like you and Jeff Howell. I want to have what you guys have. I want to be strong enough to make something of myself no matter what happens or how much effort is needed.

"Someday I want to help other people who are having a tough time in life but hunger for more—people who are willing to do what it takes. Sometimes a person just needs a helping hand to pull them up. I guess the underdog will always have a special place in my heart. When I own my own company I want to help people grow and let them know that they count for something—just like you've done for me."

"I like that, A.B.," said Mr. Stevens. "Your goals are honorable, and they obviously bring out a lot of passion in you. A vision without passion is like a new car that doesn't have any gas. It may look shiny and pretty sitting there in the driveway, but it won't get you anywhere. Passion is the fuel that will drive your vision."

Next he told me to take a minute or two and write down my career vision and why I chose it. Here's what I wrote on the first page of my new notebook:

- Career Vision: Ten years from now I will own my own construction company.
- Why: I want to amount to something, no matter what, and I want to help others amount to something, too.

There was something about writing down those words that caused me to get really stoked about the future. It felt like all the cells in my body were on fire. Affirming my commitment in writing had a powerful effect on me, and somehow it began to trigger events around me in an incredible way.

Mr. Stevens had more to say on the subject of career goals. "Now that you have a specific vision for your career, you need to put together some short-term goals that will help you start moving toward it. The two areas you need to focus on in order to advance are *skills and education*. A wide variety of skills is needed to run a construction business, and I'm going to help you out with this one. In two weeks I'm going to transfer you over to work with Andy Rodriguez, our best project manager. You'll be his apprentice, so soak up everything you can from him, kid. He's the best in the business.

"Second you need to further your education. I suggest getting a degree in construction management first, so you can learn the science behind building. And since you seem to like the idea of being the boss, it wouldn't hurt to get a masters' degree in something. How much education do you have right now, A.B.?"

I was really embarrassed to answer his question, but I was learning to own my actions so I told the truth. "Mr. Stevens, I don't even have a high school diploma because I dropped out of school when I was sixteen."

Thankfully he wasn't judgmental about this; he didn't gasp or roll his eyes, or sigh real big. In fact, my lack of education didn't seem to discourage him in the least. He simply said, "A.B. I know in the past you've struggled to stay alive and everything you've learned up to this point has been by doing. However, there is a better way to learn than just from your own experience—a much better way. We can't live long enough to learn everything we need to know simply by doing. There are only so many days in one lifetime available for learning. So you have to learn to cheat."

"You want me to become a cheater?"

He laughed when he realized I had taken him seriously. "Yes, but only in this one way: Learn from the experiences of other people and also what *they* learned from others. This gives you the benefit of many lifetimes of experience (even hundreds of years) in a very short period of time."

Mr. Stevens picked up a piece of plywood, laid it on the table, and then handed me a ruler and a pencil. Pointing to one corner of the plywood, he said, "From that corner measure three feet across the top of the board and make a mark at that point. Then measure four feet down the left side of the board and make a mark. Now from your first mark draw a line to the second mark."

As soon as I drew a line connecting the two points, he said, "Can you tell me how long that line is without measuring it?"

"I don't think so. How can anybody do that?"

"I can—and the guy I learned it from figured it out over 2,000 years ago. His name was Pythagoras, and he was a Greek mathematician. Let me show you how he did it. Multiply three times three for the three-foot side of the triangle."

I was good enough at math to figure this one out: "Nine"

"Good, he said. "Now multiply four times four for the four-foot side."

I did it. "Sixteen."

"Now add those two numbers together: that is nine plus sixteen, which equals twenty-five. Now what number multiplied by itself equals twenty-five?"

This was starting to get really confusing. "I'm not sure. Let me think about it. Uh, it's five…five times five equals twenty-five."

"Very good. Five is the square-root of twenty-five," he said. "Now let's check the theory. Measure the line; it should be five feet."

I did what Mr. Stevens said and he was right. *Man, that's like magic. I thought. There really is something to this education stuff. He was right. I'll never live long enough to learn everything on my own. I need his help, just like I needed Jeff's help.*

I needed other teachers, too. Suddenly I saw teachers in a whole new way. Furthermore, I have seen them in a different light ever since, and I've also developed an appreciation for how instrumental they are in helping us achieve our dreams. There is no such thing as a "self-made man." We all need teachers.

Mr. Stevens continued to press me on the need for education. "First you need to get your G.E.D. to complete your high school education. The local community college can help. Do you know anybody over there?"

"Why, as a matter of fact I do. She happens to work in the Admissions Department and she's a good cook, too." I said with a big grin, thinking of Juliann.

"Outstanding! It always fascinates me when people are able to develop a clear vision and start pursuing it. Things begin to fall into place."

Mr. Stevens said the first week's goal would be for me to get the ball rolling on my G.E.D. In the meantime, he would set up a meeting the following week with Andy to firm up my starting date to become Andy's apprentice in project management. He also mentioned that he thought this would be a better deal than the job I missed getting a couple of weeks ago. It would give me a much broader exposure to the construction business.

"Funny how these things work out, kid. Sometimes an event we think is a setback turns out to be a setup for something better. You thought that little mishap with you showing up late for the van was a terrible mistake, and it was, but that's not all it was. It turned out to be an opportunity as well. The more you learn to look at problems as opportunities, the faster you're going to climb the ladder of success."

> "The more you learn to look at problems
> as opportunities, the faster you're going to
> climb the ladder of success."
> —Jim Stevens

While on lunch break that afternoon I walked across the street to a pay phone and called Juliann to tell her about my new goal and ask her about the G.E.D. program at the college. She said they had classes to prepare people for the test and she would be happy to pick up the admission papers if I wanted to come by her house later and fill them out. She even said she would help me study for the test, and that if we got busy I could finish the process in a month. That would be just in time to get enrolled for the spring semester and start taking college classes. We were definitely gearing up for progress in achieving my new goal.

Juliann worked with me on preparing for the G.E.D. and I passed the test within a month. After that she helped me complete the admission process to enroll for my first courses in college: English, Economics, and History. If you would have told me a year before that I'd be going to college I would have said you were crazy, but there I was—a real "Joe College Guy."

Mr. Stevens kept his word and transferred me

over to begin working with Andy Rodriguez a couple of weeks later. He continued to meet with me every Monday morning for more than a year. During that time I was able to clarify my vision for other areas of my life and develop more goals and actions. He helped me understand that regardless of why you create a vision or what you plan to do with it, the process is pretty much the same. Here's what he taught me:

- Establish a vision of what you want to accomplish, including a compelling *why*.
- Develop a plan of action based on daily, weekly, and monthly goals.
- Write down your vision and goals.
- Look at them daily to help you stay focused, both consciously and subconsciously.

THE OLD MAN APPEARS ON THE MOUNTAIN, AND A.B. IS GIVEN THE FOURTH LAW OF THE SHOVEL

The old man appeared again around that time. I was standing at the base of a mountain—or perhaps I was only dreaming—and he was perched on the top, smiling and waving at me to join him. I immediately started to climb, but about half way up I encountered a large field of giant boulders that looked like behemoths. He was still smiling and beckoning to me.

After struggling over the first gigantic rock, I felt drained and exhausted. When I reached the other side I was trapped in a dead end. Surrounded by huge overhangs with no way out, I wondered whether or not I should go on. Suddenly he appeared beside me and then we were back at the base where I had started.

"Look up," he said. "There are several paths to the top but you must find the one that is best for you. First, be still and study the landscape before you choose your path. Otherwise you might work hard only to find you're at a dead end and need to start over."

As we stood there gazing up at the distant mountaintop, I began to notice there were several ways to get there. Some were much longer and steeper than others. There was one particular path that appeared to have obstacles, but I believed they could be overcome. So I started climbing again. The old man was already up at the top again, shouting words of encouragement. He kept reminding me to look upward and keep moving, even when the path seemed too difficult.

I was a little over half way there, when suddenly there was a thundering noise and rocks began to tumble down around me. I hugged the boulder in front of me as a huge ground-shaking landslide hurtled past me. Any one of those rocks could have crushed me. When the commotion stopped and silence returned I was still standing, but shaking with fear. I looked up and the old man was still there—and he was laughing.

How can he be laughing? I could have been crushed by those boulders. Why does he think it's funny? Suddenly I became angry—and tired and frustrated. My urge to quit was quite strong.

He suddenly appeared beside me and said, "What doesn't kill you makes you stronger, kid. Life is filled with risks so get used to it, and know that within crisis lies both danger and opportunity. You get to choose which one to focus on. Are you going to quit or are you going to keep climbing?"

> **"Within crisis lies both danger and opportunity. You get to choose which one to focus on. Are you going to quit or are you going to keep climbing?"—The Old Man**

My legs were shaking as I walked over to a nearby rock and sat down. I leaned back and looked up. At first, to my dismay, I saw that the entire route I had picked earlier was gone. Then I heard the old man say, "There is a way to the top of this mountain—and any other challenge that might seem like a mountain. Keep visualizing where you want to go and keep moving. No matter how difficult it might seem, your path will be revealed."

I was afraid the loose rocks would start another slide, so I had to move very slowly at first. Suddenly I caught a glimpse of a solid path buried just below the loose rocks in front of me. I took a few steps and caught another glimpse…and then another…and another. The path was right there in the midst of the debris from the slide.

Encouraged, I continued to press onward. Finding the path became easier as I climbed higher and higher, and soon I was standing at the top of the mountain with the old man, who was beaming at me. He seemed quite proud that his student had mastered the task.

We sat quietly for a while gazing out at a majestic vista filled with beautiful mountains and lush green valleys. I felt exhausted and exhilarated at the same time. I turned to him and said, "Thank you for showing me the way."

"I didn't choose your path, you did. All I did was encourage you to keep looking upward and challenge you to continue moving forward. You had to find your own path—and you had to muster the passion and courage within your own heart to keep climbing, even in the face of a deadly landslide. I knew you could do it. I believe in you."

There was a feeling of warm acceptance in his smile that I had never felt before. It was something I'd always wanted from my own father but never received.

"Keep your eyes fixed on where you want to go, my son," said the old man, as if sensing what I was feeling. "Allow the passion in your heart to carry you."

Then suddenly I was wide awake and full of energy, and there was that familiar smell of something burnt. Sure enough, the Four Law was engraved on the shovel.

IV. Visualize Your Future

From that moment on my life had purpose. I started getting up every day with a vision and the passion to move toward it. Sadly, people with no vision get up each morning and repeat the same things they did the day before, while still hoping for different results that never come. That, my friend, is insanity. I'm grateful to have been shown a better way. I knew then that I was going somewhere, and I have known it every day since. This is one of the greatest feelings in the world—knowing your purpose, seeing your vision, and enjoying the journey.

6

EXTRA EFFORT PAYS

We walked together in silence for a few minutes, as Mr. Lincoln allowed me time to absorb the full meaning of the conversation and the lessons he was trying to teach me.

Then we headed back to the office. As we approached the building I looked up and marveled at the architecture of what I considered the most beautiful structure in the city. I complimented Mr. Lincoln on his incredible work of art.

"It all began with a vision. I saw it in here first," he said, pointing to the side of his head. "Whatever you see with your mind can be achieved with your hands if you have a little faith and a whole lot of gumption. And I had a lot of gumption back in those days...still do."

We took the elevator to the top of the building, where we could look out at the city in every direction. From there, he shared with me more of the visions he had for the future.

To the east of the city there was a large shopping mall under construction, with a huge water reservoir and solar panels that would produce enough geothermal and solar energy to generate one hundred percent of the electricity the mall needed year-round. He said it was going to be the first retail structure of its kind in North America that would be entirely energy sufficient.

To the west there was a newly constructed sports complex, complete with soccer fields, baseball and softball diamonds, a skateboard park, swimming pool, three basketball courts, and a nine-hole golf course that was lighted so people could play at night. Mr. Lincoln's construction company had built the complex so the kids in the city would have a place where they could get involved in healthy, wholesome activities. He said the complex was also going to employ over three hundred young people from the surrounding community on a part-time basis.

To the south there was a senior citizens' retirement center that was almost complete. This wasn't like any old folks' home I had ever seen. It looked more like a high-dollar resort you might see somewhere in Florida or Southern California. Mr. Lincoln said he had already worked out a deal with the merchants association to hire on a part-time basis many of the senior citizens who were going to live at the center. A shuttle service would provide transportation back and forth to the mall and other places around town, so the seniors could continue to come and go and earn a livelihood, even into their advanced years.

To the north of the city there was a new residential community under construction. A.B. said the houses in this community were designed to be energy efficient and they were priced very reasonably, especially for first-time homebuyers, who were mostly young couples with small children.

As he gazed out over the city, A.B. said, "Our company philosophy is driven by what I call the 'Four Rs of Business': Reduce, Reuse, Recycle, and Reinvest.

"First, we continually look for ways to work smarter through *reducing* our overhead and improving our environmental impact. This applies to cutting the costs of the raw materials we use and reducing the amount of toxic emissions or waste that might be created at our jobsites. We take careful measures to ensure that the water, air, and soil are unaffected by what we do.

"We *reuse* as much leftover material as we can, in order to save money and natural resources. It doesn't make sense to keep filling landfills with materials that can be reused. We have developed partnerships with other organizations to help us *recycle* metals such as copper, magnesium, chromium, and aluminum, so we can reuse these valuable resources over and over again.

"Most importantly, none of us, including myself, receive exorbitant salaries or corporate perks. Instead we *reinvest* our profits back into the growth of our employees and community, because we realize that our most valuable asset at Lincoln Construction is people—our human capital."

> **"Our company philosophy is driven by what I call the 'Four Rs of Business': Reduce, Reuse, Recycle, and Reinvest."**
> **—A.B. Lincoln**

Now I knew I had met a truly great man. Looking back at that first day and knowing what I know now about A.B. Lincoln, I can't help but think every leader in America could learn something from him. He felt that private citizens and companies should be responsible for investing in our communities and helping underprivileged people instead of depending on the government. He said too many people look to the government for handouts or bailouts, and this eventually results in feelings of entitlement and a lack of personal accountability.

A.B. Lincoln believed with every fiber of his being in the sentiments expressed by President John F. Kennedy: "Ask not what your country can do for you, but what you can do for your country."

A.B. had a vision for the future but he also cared deeply about his community. He was tireless in his efforts to leave a positive mark on the world. Instead of looking at how life is today and asking *why*, he always looked at what might happen tomorrow and asked *why not*.

A.B. SHARES WITH JASON THE STORY OF HIS ONGOING EDUCATION AND WHAT HE LEARNED FROM ANDY RODRIGUEZ

As I said earlier, Mr. Stevens continued to mentor me and I kept my nose to the grindstone for many years. The classes I took in construction management at the community college helped me understand the science behind building structures that were strong and safe. The education I got from Andy Rodriguez was also invaluable. In the beginning, it was a little strange. Andy had a lazy eye that seemed to look off in the other direction while you were talking to him. At first I had difficulty tracking him during a conversation because I didn't know which eye he was looking at me with, and I didn't know which of his eyes to look back at. One day I asked him which eye I should talk to. He simply laughed and said, "Either one, A.B., I can listen to you with both of them."

Andy was one of the most intelligent men I had ever met. He knew the construction business inside and out, and he knew about a whole lot of other things, too. One day I asked him, "Andy, how'd you get so smart?" He grinned and replied that he had fallen in love with reading books when he was younger and it changed his life. I told him I didn't like to read much and that it took a lot of discipline for me to stay focused on my coursework in college.

Andy said reading was also difficult for him at first. In fact, it was almost impossible. In grade school his teachers initially told his parents that he was "intellectually challenged," which was another way of saying he was retarded. They told his parents he would never be able to mentally perform like the other kids, but his mother refused to accept this diagnosis. She took Andy to specialists, who determined that he had dyslexia, a learning disability resulting from differences in how the brain processes written and spoken language. Although dyslexia is thought to be the result of a neurological difference in the brain, it's not an intellectual disability. This meant there was nothing wrong with Andy's intelligence, although he did have to take extra reading classes in order to learn how to process information in a different way.

Andy said he had to work harder than the other kids to learn how to read and comprehend the information, and that in the process he fell in love with learning. He read everything he could get his hands on, which helped him to expand his vocabulary and his ability to communicate with people on all levels. He was able to go to college and earn a degree in civil engineering. After that he continued to read over fifty books a year. It was one of his greatest passions.

Andy challenged me to read more. "A.B., if you want to be a great leader you must be a great reader. If you read ten pages a day, in one year you will have read thirty to forty books. Do this for five years and watch the doors of opportunity open. It doesn't matter what topics you choose—if you read two hundred books on any topic, you'll be considered an expert."

Andy believed that reading was a good way to stretch your mind. He told me that once your mind has been stretched, it rarely goes back to its original dimensions. Speaking of stretching, he seemed to constantly find ways to challenge me to move beyond my limitations and grow both personally and professionally.

He even talked me into skydiving, because he believed it would help me face some of my greatest fears.

He was an instructor at the local skydiving club, and I'll never forget the first time I went with him. It was a beautiful fall day and the leaves on the maples and oak trees were at their peak with vibrant colors of red, yellow, and orange. I figured it was a perfect day to jump out of an airplane!

I was a lot more scared than I expected to be. "Don't worry about it. You're going to be fine," said Andy. He had loads of confidence. "Just go for it! You already know what to do."

His reassurance didn't help much. My stomach felt like it was in my throat, and I remember thinking that I was glad he was a skydiving instructor instead of a psychologist specializing in dealing with fear. He would have had his license revoked.

I was about to get on an airplane headed for 15,000 feet. Then I would do a solo, pull-your-own-ripcord jump with a free fall of 10,000 feet, which would take about sixty-five seconds. When Andy told me I already knew what to do, he was referring to the four-hour course we had gone through that morning, showing us how to count, how to pull the ripcord, and then how to jettison our chute if it got tangled, torn, or didn't open for some reason. We also had to watch an hour-long video of an attorney citing case law and contractual reasons why the company would not be liable for the death of anyone in the class—because we had voluntarily signed up to die! *What was I doing?* I thought. *Had I gone totally crazy?*

As we ascended to our jump altitude I was amazed at how high up we were. At 3,000 feet—approximately one-fifth of where we were headed—the pilot told us to look out the window and see what the landing area looked like. Whatever part of me was not afraid caught up with the rest of me when I looked out the window.

When we got to 15,000 feet, I couldn't recognize anything on the ground. It was just an ocean of colors. I said a quick prayer and put my fate in God's hands, since I thought for sure I was going to die anyway. Moving carefully toward the door, I looked into Andy's eyes. Then I looked out of the open door and made the instantaneous decision to jump.

The first thing I felt was the force of the wind in my face. At a fall rate of 120 miles per hour, the wind is definitely strong enough to get your attention. But in about ten seconds I lost all sensation of falling and actually felt like I was flying.

After free-falling about 10,000 feet, I pulled the ripcord. There was some movement in the lines and cords, and then there was a jolt. I looked up expecting to see a tangled mess of a chute. I was ready to jettison it and try to open the spare. But a miracle had occurred. My chute looked picture perfect. I couldn't believe it. I was probably going to live. I adjusted the chute and retrieved the guidelines, and began to look around.

I was floating in the most amazing state of quiet I had ever experienced. I could see vibrant colors below, mountains in the distance, a beautiful lake, and a blue sky above me. I had never felt the combination of freedom and serenity that I did at that moment. It was a spiritual experience and I didn't want it to end. It felt like a bird must feel, just soaring in the wind without a care in the world, enjoying God's creation. The ride down only lasted about ten minutes and then I was ready to do it again!

It was incredibly exciting. I told Andy that after jumping out of that airplane I felt like I could do anything. He laughed and said jokingly, "Great! Next week I'm going to take you bull riding!" We went over and sat down beside the hangar and watched the planes taking off.

Andy became serious for a moment and then said, "Life is like jumping out of an airplane. You must overcome your fear or you will never go out the door. How do you overcome fear? You take action. And once you do, your fear transforms into a completely new experience. What was previously dreadful becomes exhilarating. Where you once experienced paralyzing fear, you now experience freedom. This is how all significant growth and learning occurs in life. It will help you develop confidence and competence. If you don't learn anything else from your experience today, remember these three simple concepts:

- Face your fear
- Take action
- Be willing grow

"The difference between winners and losers in life, Jason, is that winners are willing to do this—over and over and over again—in the small things as well as the big ones."

> **"Life is like jumping out of an airplane. You must overcome your fear or you will never go out the door. How do you overcome fear? You take action."**
> **—Andy Rodriguez**

Andy had the same approach for both work and play. In fact, they were the same to him. He totally enjoyed life and lived with enthusiasm and courage. If someone asked him to do something, he did it passionately and always went the extra mile. "It's really pretty simple," Andy said. "Do the very best you can wherever you are, and with whatever you have. Do anything less and you're only average. If you look at the difference between the performance of world champions in sports and those who fall short of the goal, the margin is often very slim—sometimes only a fraction of a second. The winners are the people who are willing to put in a little extra effort to win—like Jeff Howell does when he rinses the fat off his cottage cheese to gain an extra edge in triathlons!

"You're not the first guy Mr. Stevens mentored and coached on Monday mornings, A.B. When I came here as a young man, I was a bigger mess than you were, but he saw something in me that I didn't see in myself. I'll never forget what he did for me, and my loyalty runs deep. Sure I could go somewhere else and make more money, but it's not just about the money. Don't just satisfy people; make the extra effort to *wow* them! When you *wow* people, it creates loyalty, which will have a monumental impact on both your business and personal success. When you treat a person like they are important, you'll not only gain a friend, that person will voluntarily become part of your personal sales force. They will actually sell *you* to others!"

Apparently he was right, because Andy had more business opportunities than anybody I have ever known.

Andy's teaching helped me in many ways. By learning to "go the extra mile" like Andy, I developed a reputation in the business as someone who did top quality work. Opportunities seemed to just show up for me.

At first I worked on the side with Andy in his subcontracting business. Eventually I got into the position where I could pick and choose my own side jobs, which were pretty lucrative for a young guy still in college. Every bit of the business that came to me was by word-of-mouth referrals because of the quality of work I performed. As Andy always said, "Going the extra mile makes sense in terms of dollars and cents."

As the years went by, Jason, I became more and more successful in the construction business. I worked hard and saved my money until I was finally able to buy my first house—a modest three-bedroom place over on Magnolia...for some reason I always liked the name of that street. It was a little place but it felt like a mansion.

The first night I slept in my new house I reflected on the time years before when I was sleeping by the railroad track, and how far my life had come since then. I looked at the blade of my trusty old shovel and recollected the lessons from each of the laws written on it. By that time I no longer carried the shovel to work with me. Instead, I placed it like a trophy in the corner of my living room. Years later I moved it to my office where it rightfully belongs.

THE OLD MAN SHOWS UP AGAIN, AND ANOTHER LAW IS ETCHED INTO THE SHOVEL

It had been years since I'd seen the old man, and I thought maybe he had moved on or forgotten about me. Then one night he appeared again. He was covered in dust from head to toe. He looked right at me and said, "No, A.B. I haven't forgotten you."

Okay. He was reading my mind again.

"Excuse the dust. I have been down in a mine watching another friend enjoying his great discovery. He bought a mine from a man who had given up on it because the going got tough and he didn't think it was worth it to continue. Ironically, the former owner was very close to the mother lode when he quit. When my friend purchased the mine, he went to the extra effort of seeking the advice of a geologist. He and the geologist spent a lot of time poking, prodding, and testing dirt to find the best places to dig. Their extra effort took a lot of sweat and patience but it paid off.

"I really enjoyed watching his face when they uncovered that rich, beautiful vein of gold. You are like that miner, A.B. You have been willing to learn from others and go the extra mile. I have watched you stretch and grow every step of the way—and speaking of which, that airplane jump was pretty magnificent, even by my standards. You have learned and practiced the next Law of the Shovel well, and I am pleased with what you have accomplished. Continue pursuing your passion and get ready, because for you the sky's the limit, kid!"

He looked at me with a mischievous grin and a twinkle in his eye—and then he was gone, just evaporated into thin air.

I woke up the next morning and smiled to myself when I thought about what he had said. That old man was something else. I couldn't figure him out, but I believed without a doubt that he cared a lot about me. I went over to the shovel to read the new law that had been etched into the blade.

V. Extra Effort Pays

Things were good in my life at that point, Jason. I'm not saying every day was a mountain top experience, because it wasn't. But you've got to have some valleys in order to appreciate the peaks. And as Andy used to say, "After the ecstasy, you still have the dirty dishes and laundry to do." In other words, no matter how grand life becomes, the mundane still exists, and that's okay because true success is the product of the many little, boring, and seemingly insignificant things performed over and over in the ordinary moments of life. *Hmmm...come to think of it, there are no ordinary moments.*

> **"After the ecstasy, you still have the dirty dishes and laundry to do."**
> **—Andy Rodriquez**

7

LEARN TO LOVE

Mr. Lincoln wanted to take the stairs back down so we could stop and explore the company's Learning Resources Center on the sixth floor. It was stocked with almost as many books as a public library—everything from classic novels to books on leadership, communication, construction management, financial planning, engineering, geology, history, sociology, and anthropology. There were also books on spirituality, building relationships, parenting, and health.

Tables and chairs were scattered throughout the room for discussion groups to meet. I could see from the sign-up sheets posted on the wall that there were various groups that met each week, including the "book of the month" club, a parenting group, and a conversational Spanish class. Mr. Lincoln participated in a couple of the groups and encouraged everyone in the company to spend time here learning and growing, both personally and professionally. It seemed too good to be true, especially in view of my background.

JASON SHARES HIS FAMILY HISTORY
WITH A.B.

Mr. Lincoln, you don't know how lucky I feel to be a part of this company. My life wasn't always this good. As an African-American, I really appreciate your Resource Center because I am only a couple of generations removed from my ancestors, who didn't have the opportunities I have. Actually I'm half African-American and half Caucasian; my mother was black and my father was white. He left us when I was five years old and my mother raised my little sister and me by herself. My father remarried and his new wife didn't want anything to do with us stepchildren, especially since we were "colored."

My mother worked two jobs and taught us to work hard, too. She instilled in us the idea that all things are possible in America. She raked and scraped to put away money for college so we could get the education that she didn't have. She never once bad-mouthed my father, but she had every right to because he was a worthless piece of "you-know-what" who never called or offered any support for his kids. I've never understood how anyone could be so cold-hearted or indifferent toward his own flesh and blood. Even though I haven't heard from him in more than fifteen years, I still have disdain for the man.

MR. LINCOLN SHARES HIS DISAPPOINTMENTS WITH JASON AND HOW HE OVERCAME THEM

It's unfortunate, Jason, that you experienced so much disappointment with your father. There's no excuse for how he treated you and your little sister, but don't let him pull you down so low as to hate him. Ultimately it will only hurt you and the people you love. I know this well because I had to learn some painful lessons in that area myself.

I carried a grudge against my old man for many years. Funny thing about carrying a grudge, it's like taking poison and expecting that some other s.o.b. will die. My anger was killing me and I didn't even know it. I became overly critical of myself and everyone around me. If someone dared treat me with even a hint of disrespect, they would sure be sorry. I didn't just level *with* people; I *leveled them*! When things went my way I was a good natured, fun-loving guy everyone loved to

be around. But when my critical nature became un-
leashed, holy cow, look out!

Juliann was instrumental in helping me to see
how this behavior was sabotaging my own happiness
and success in my personal and business relationships.
As you probably suspected, our friendship grew into
something deeper. In fact, I fell head-over-heels in love
with her during that first year and I believe she felt the
same about me. I must admit I was pretty clueless in
matters of love back then, but she was a patient teacher.
We spent hours talking and sharing our dreams. How
sweet it was to be young and in love—as a matter-of-
fact I still feel that way about her.

My stress level was pretty high in those days because I was working and going to school full time. Bless
her heart, Juliann would listen to me rant and rave
about issues at work and the frustrations I experienced
in class with my instructors and fellow students. The
more stressed I was, the more critical I became. Sometimes my fuse was so short I'm surprised she could
stand to be around me. At first, she only had to listen
to me vent and criticize others when they didn't act the
way I thought they should. But eventually she experienced the brunt of my critical nature firsthand when I
turned on her over something relatively insignificant
and stupid. That's when she sat me down and initiated
a "Things Need to Change" talk with me.

"I love you, A.B., and my heart aches for you when I see you going through these episodes of anger and criticism. You're a wonderful man and ninety-eight percent of the time you're a genuine pleasure to be around, but that other two percent is just horrible! This behavior has become intolerable. I will not sit idly by and watch your anger destroy your happiness, or mine. It's time to deal with it—that's if you think our future together is worth it. How about it? Which do you choose—your anger or *us*?'

Talk about a slap in the face of reality. I couldn't believe she was issuing an ultimatum. Part of me wanted to start yelling and tell her what she could do with her ultimatum. But another part of me, the saner part I reckon, realized that she was offering me the best deal of my life. Let's see, my anger or this gorgeous woman who adored me? It was easy to decide. I chose a future with Juliann.

It didn't happen overnight, but I gradually turned my anger into compassion by starting to think about people and situations in a different way. Juliann regularly reminded me that the best way to change your life is to change how you think. She explained that people didn't purposely cross me or get up in the morning thinking, "How can I screw A.B. Lincoln today?" People are imperfect creatures and they make mistakes. My problem was that I was a perfectionist and I also took things too personally. Consequently I stayed about half-cocked and ready to nail people to the wall if they screwed up. Back then I had a lot to learn about "winning friends and influencing people."

> "People are imperfect creatures and they make mistakes. My problem was that I was a perfectionist and I also took things too personally. I've found that life just works better when we don't hold grudges against people."—A.B. Lincoln

First I had to learn how to forgive God for not creating a perfect world. I had to forgive my parents for not being there for me. I had to forgive people who didn't even know I was still holding a grudge against them. Most of all I had to forgive myself and that was probably the hardest thing of all.

JASON ASKS AN IMPORTANT QUESTION

Forgiveness is a tough one for me, too, Mr. Lincoln. I know the Bible says we're supposed to forgive and forget, but how do you do it? Are we supposed to have amnesia all of a sudden or something?"

AND A.B. RESPONDS

Actually the Bible doesn't say "forgive and forget," Jason. It says that when God forgives us, He no longer *remembers* the offense. There is a difference between the two. Of course God doesn't forget and neither can we. In forgiving others we simply make a choice not to remember the offense any longer. This means choosing to let it go—and sometimes it's necessary to let it go repeatedly until we are finally free of it.

The act of forgiveness doesn't always produce a warm, fuzzy feeling. Furthermore, you don't even have to like a person to forgive him. Forgiveness is not for *their* sake, it's for *ours*. The real question is, "Do you love yourself enough to do it?" I've found that life just works better when we don't hold grudges against people. It sure has made me an easier person to be around. Juliann will attest to that.

And speaking of Juliann, she has been a great gift to me—much more than I probably deserved. We dated throughout those early years and finally got married during my first year of graduate school. She is without a doubt one of the most effective leaders I have ever met. She continues to build a successful network marketing business with thousands of independent consultants, who all share an amazing loyalty to her. I think the people in her organization would walk through fire for Juliann. If you asked her to tell you the secret of her success, she would probably shrug and say it's simply based on a four-letter word—*love*. She believes the best way to lead is to genuinely love and care about people.

And that, my friend, is the driving force behind Lincoln Construction Company. We *love* people. I'm not saying everybody gets together for a group hug and sings Kumbaya at the end of the day, but we do our best to let people know we respect them and value their contribution. When new people are hired we spend time making them feel welcome, as I have with you today. Mentors are also assigned to assist all of our new associates. You'll meet your mentor tomorrow, and he'll work with you regularly to help you get acclimated and trained efficiently for your work responsibilities.

You're important to us, Jason, and not because of the color of your skin, your socio-economic background, your academic pedigree, your religion, or your political affiliations. We carefully chose you to work for Lincoln Construction because of your *character*. We do an extensive background search on all of our associates, and we look for qualities such as community involvement, acts of charity, generosity, selfless living, and passion. I already know quite a bit about you, like those times when you volunteered to ring the bell for the Salvation Army when you were a kid—and the time you offered to donate a kidney to a sick classmate in high school. And yes, I know about that big brawl you got into over in Hendersonville defending one of your friends against a gang of bullies. You're not perfect but you have a tremendous heart. You should fit right in here at Lincoln Construction.

It was getting late in the day and I could tell by his body language that A.B. was getting ready to end our time together. "It's been a genuine pleasure spending this time with you, Jason," he said.

"Mr. Lincoln, I just want to say thank you. If I walked out that door right now and never worked a day for you, I would always feel indebted for what you have already done for me. Yes sir, this has been a real learning experience. I have always wondered how my father could be so cold, while my mom was so devoted and made so many sacrifices. Now I realize the answer to both those questions is the same: *love*. The *absence* of love allowed my father to shut us out of his life— whereas, *love* was the driving force in everything my mother did.

"You have cleared up a lot of the mystery and confusion for me today. I expect my life will be different from this point on because you have taken the time to share your life story with me. Please don't laugh when I say this, Mr. Lincoln, but I want to be just like you."

A.B. Lincoln looked straight into my eyes and didn't speak for a moment. "What you've just said touches me very deeply. We never know when we open up to others how they'll respond. And I know it has been a risk for you to open up to me. Thank you for the gift of sharing. I guess it's safe to say we can "call it even." We are fortunate to have had this time together. Today we began by sharing our history. Tomorrow we'll start making history together, my young friend.

Speaking of the future…we host a dinner party at our house the first Friday night of every month for our newly hired associates. This will give you a chance to meet Juliann and get to know our twins, Caleb and Joshua, and their younger sister Alicia. They will be home from college that night. I like to think they got most of their mother's good qualities and very few of my bad ones. Anyway I think you will all like each other."

There was one final question I was burning to ask. "Oh! There's one last thing, sir…my curiosity is bothering me. Did you ever see the old man again?"

THE OLD MAN APPEARS FOR
THE LAST TIME, AND A.B. RECEIVES
THE FINAL LAW OF THE SHOVEL

"Oh yes. The very last time the old man appeared to me, we were seated at a table in a lake cabin. We had been talking and he invited me into the living room. As I was walking over to sit down on a sofa in front of a roaring fire in the fireplace, something moving on the floor to the right caught my eye. I looked down and there was a snake about two feet long slithering toward the middle of the room. By automatic reflex, I jumped straight up and came down hard with both feet on the snake. One foot landed near its head and the other near the middle of its body. Then I jumped back and looked down at the writhing snake, as it curled round and around, rolled on its back, and then flopped over on its belly and laid still.

The old man came over and picked up the snake tenderly in both hands and looked at me. There were tears in his eyes and I detected sadness in his voice. "Why did you do that?"

"What else could I do? It was a snake. It could have been poisonous, and it might have bitten someone, especially me." Somehow he made me feel defensive and foolish at the same time.

"Her name is Samantha, and any mouse who decides to take up residence in the house eventually becomes her dinner. She has her place here, and she is better than a cat when it comes to patrolling the house and controlling the mice. She doesn't leave hair balls and I don't have to put out food or water for her, either. Also she is quiet and never demands to be petted. Besides, I'm allergic to cats. Samantha has been with me for a long time," the old man said. He held the limp snake close to his chest, as if willing his own life force into her small body.

I could see blood oozing from near her tail and also from her mouth, which is never a good sign. Suddenly I felt guilty—like I had done something wrong. But at the same time I felt a sense of righteous indignation. Then I became angry. "Hey, it's just a snake, and the only good snake is a dead snake."

The old man looked at me intently, and for the first time I saw disappointment in his eyes. I knew immediately I had said the wrong thing.

"The statement you just made reveals the essence of all prejudice, A.B. Everything in the Universe has its place, whether it is a snake or a human being. When you don't understand and accept people of different color, ethnic origin, or beliefs, you fear them and strike out violently. You are afraid of all snakes because some of them can bite and harm you. However there are places where people live with deadly cobras in their immediate environment, but they don't spend time chasing or killing them, or living in fear. They understand that snakes kill rats, which carry horrible diseases harmful to humans. So, in essence, what you might perceive to be dangerous, they understand and accept to be beneficial.

"You must learn to deal with your prejudice, A.B., which is driven by fear. It results in anger, which in turn causes others around you to suffer because of your violent outbursts, especially those you love the most. Love is the one thing that overcomes fear and anger. Love will move you beyond merely being successful and into a life of true significance. So spend your time learning to love instead of looking for snakes to kill."

I began to question whether I could ever again kill a snake, either literally or symbolically, and when I picked up the shovel the final law had been etched into the blade.

VI. Learn to Love

It was a defining moment in my life—when I made a conscious choice to stop wasting time "killing snakes" and instead start investing my time in building a life of significance. The more I have awakened to my own prejudices, fear, and anger throughout the years, the more time and energy I have had for the things I love. The opposite of hate and anger is love and acceptance. My last visit with the old man helped me understand that we must let go of one in order to fully experience the other. Jason, it's no coincidence that we are in the construction business. Let's build something significant together, my friend, and let's do it with love.

Jason's Epilogue

Over twenty-five years have come and gone since my first day at Lincoln Construction. A.B. and I spent a lot of quality time together, as he took me under his wing and taught me the construction business. I also became very good friends with his kids, who treated me like part of the family. In fact, I spent many holidays at their house enjoying Juliann's wonderful cooking and warm hospitality. Both she and A.B. treated me like a son.

Then one day A.B. called Caleb, Joshua, Alicia and me into his office to discuss his deteriorating health. We knew he had battled prostate cancer several years before but we thought it was in remission. Apparently his condition had changed. He told us that he had just been through another series of tests and the prognosis wasn't good. The cancer had returned and metastasized in his bones. The doctors gave him a year at the most.

He had been mentoring the four of us for some time to assume the leadership of the company when he retired, and now we needed to accelerate that process. The plan was for each of us to be responsible for a specific area of the business. This should be an indication of what kind of leader A.B. Lincoln was—it took four people to "fill his shoes."

A.B. died as he had lived, with character and courage. He never complained and he showed up every day at work with a positive attitude and a smile. Throughout his last pain-filled days, his major concern was for his family and friends, and *our* sense of loss. Even to the very end, he was one of the most gracious and loving men I have ever met. He was also a man of great vision.

Shortly after he died, I attended a ribbon-cutting ceremony for a special education school and community center he had endowed years before. After the ceremony one young journalist quipped, "It's too bad the old guy didn't live to see this." Juliann overheard him and adamantly responded, "Oh, but A.B. did see it, as he saw so many things. If he hadn't, it wouldn't be here today." She had a tear in her eye and a smile on her face that caused her to glow like an angel. I have never seen a woman filled with such love and respect for her husband. *I hope someday I deserve a woman who loves me that much.*

One of the greatest honors I ever received was when he asked me to deliver the eulogy at his funeral "Jason, you have been like a son to me, and it would mean a lot if you would give an uplifting talk at the celebration of my life." *Celebration* was the word he preferred to use when talking about his funeral.

During the service, which was attended by over a thousand people whose lives he had touched, I told a couple of humorous stories about A.B. I also shared what a kind, honorable man he was and how he touched the life of every person he encountered in a positive way. I have never met anyone with such class in my life. He got it! He truly understood what made a man rich—faith, family, and friends were his most prized possessions. This was a man of success *and* significance. After the service I stood at his grave and put my arms around Juliann, Alicia, Caleb and Joshua as we held each other and wept. Afterward, I just couldn't bring myself to leave with the others, so I walked Juliann back to the car and told her I would be over to the house later.

I was standing alone in the road waving goodbye, and as I looked back at A.B.'s grave I saw an old man standing at his tombstone with his head down. I walked up behind him and without turning around he said, "Jason, let's take a walk." *Oh-my-god! This was him! This was the old man that A.B. had told me about in his stories.* Honestly, I never thought the guy was real. I don't know how I knew it was him, but I knew. There he was in living color…and I wasn't even dreaming…I think.

"A.B. loved you like a son, Jason," said the old man. "And you have made both of us proud because you learned the Laws of the Shovel and have lived them well. He was very gracious in teaching them to you, and now I have a request. Laws are important because of the direction and substance they provide for our lives. How successful would a person be at winning a game if he had no idea what the rules were? How successful would someone be at reaching a destination if she had no map, no directions, no compass, or no discernable road signs? Could you build a house without a set of plans? Direct a stage play without a script?

Life may be likened to a game with rules, a journey with a destination, a house built with a plan, or a stage play that follows a script. Underneath the specific plans for every game, each journey, all houses, and every successful stage play, there are laws that must be known and followed if success is to be achieved.

"Ignorance or avoidance of these laws results in chaos and confusion, because without them human experiences are reduced to randomness or default. In every waking moment, people are either creating or altering their future, either by conscious intention or by accident. Jason, by choosing to follow these laws you have chosen to create a life based on *conscious intention*. Now I ask you to pass the Laws of the Shovel on to others. It will be A.B. Lincoln's legacy and yours, too."

After he spoke those words, the old man walked down the hill and vanished. I don't know if I'll ever see him again or not, but I have my suspicions. Here again are the Laws of the Shovel as they were given to me. If they worked for us, they'll work for you. And who knows, some day when you least expect it the old man just might pay you a visit, too—because when the student is ready the teacher will appear!

THE LAWS OF THE SHOVEL

I. Show Up

Show up every day with a shovel, a positive attitude, and a smile. Show others you're willing to roll up your sleeves and go to work with genuine passion for what you do. This combination will open many doors of opportunity for success.

II. Habits Make or Break You

Create the habits today that will produce the life you want tomorrow. Don't leave success to chance—

begin today to create the habits that will help you get from where you are to where you want to be.

III. Own Your Actions

Take responsibility for your life by owning up to your actions without making excuses or blaming others. Be willing to learn from your failures and maintain a spirit of humility in building the collaboration you will need from others to achieve success in the future.

IV. Visualize Your Future

Develop a clear vision of what your future will be and set specific goals to get there. Write these down and take actions to move you closer and closer toward success each day. Remember, a mountain must be moved one shovelful at a time.

V. Extra Effort Pays

Be committed to exceeding the expectations of others and develop a reputation of going the extra mile. When you establish the habit of extra effort, success will be your lifelong companion.

VI. Learn to Love

Begin to view love as a verb rather than a noun, because love is an action. Practice forgiveness for those who fail to meet your expectations, and acceptance of those who are different than you. In doing so, you will move from being a person of success to becoming a person of significance.

THE END

Acknowledgements

Baker

Thanks to my loving, patient, independent and most supportive wife Meghann for feeding me and making sure I have color coordinated clothes on when I leave the house. Thanks to my kids for turning out alright so I don't have to worry anymore. Thanks to Tom my partner for his patience with this "ultravert" of a person he refers to me as. Thanks to those who believed in us. Thanks to Bob Reed who is never too big to talk to a little guy.

Thank you God for always being there even outside my dreams and thanks for teaching me to be still so I can hear you.

Tom

Writing a book takes a team of dedicated, skilled

people to pull the concept together to turn it into a reality. We have been very fortunate to have such a team working with us on *The Shovel.* Thanks to Bob and Cleone Reed our publishers. Your support and friendship through the many years have been invaluable. Your cheerful, positive attitudes make it a genuine pleasure to work with you both. Thanks to Jessica Bryan, one of the best editors on the planet, for your determination to take a couple of Oklahoman guys and get rid of the "slang" that we seem to unconsciously slip into our writing. Your patience and dedication to excellence are simply astounding.

Thanks to Baker for being my business partner, best friend, personal physician, and much, much more. Thank you, Meghann, for putting up with all of the late nights we spend writing and trying to figure out how to change the world. You are an angel!

A very special thanks to my son Todd and daughter-in-law Dana for your unwavering love and support throughout the years. I am richly blessed to have you both in my life. To my grandsons Tyler and Paul, I dedicate this book to you. Your generation holds the keys to the future of our nation. I love you immensely and commit to do everything I can to help prepare you to be great leaders.

Most of all, thanks to God for the great things He has done and will continue to do in each of our lives.

About the Authors:

Baker Fore

Known as "Dr. Fore" to his patients and "Baker" to his friends, he lives in Southern Oklahoma with his beautiful wife Meghann. Together, they raise cats, dogs, and longhorn cows; as well as children and grandchildren, who love to visit their ranch often.

In the 1970s, Dr. Fore developed a clinic and hospital in rural New Mexico; in the 1980s, he established urgent care centers throughout Oklahoma City: in the 1990s, he was an Emergency Room physician and he created a wellness/occupational center in Ardmore, Oklahoma. In 2006, he opened the first pain management facility in Southern Oklahoma.

Baker's current goal in life is to give people the

tools they need to better themselves. He believes in teaching others to fish, rather than giving them a fish—but he is not above offering a helping hand to someone willing to give their best effort. He is now changing lives rather than just saving them. Baker Fore is also the author of *Life Sucks, So Get Rich!*

Tom Massey

Tom Massey is a leader in the field of personal and organizational performance. He is an internationally known author and speaker who has spent more than two decades sharing his principle-centered philosophy and performance strategies with diverse groups—from highly successful business leaders to world-class athletes. He is the founder of several businesses and currently serves as President for Pacesetters Consulting Group, Inc.

Tom is the author of six books on personal growth and leadership development, published by Robert D. Reed Publishers:

- *How Bad Do You REALLY Want It? Getting from Where You Are to Where You Want to Go!*

- *The ABC's of Successful Living: Getting What You REALLY Want!*

- *The ABC's of Total Health: Practical Tips for Abundant Living*

- *The ABC's of Effective Leadership: Managing from the Heart*

- *Ten Commitments for Building High Performance Teams*

- *Ten Commitments for Men*

Tom Massey can be contacted at www.TomMasseyInc.com.

About the Collaborative Effort of the Authors

This work is a unique collaboration of stories and life principles learned cumulatively by the authors over a span of more than seventy years. During the writing of this book, Baker Fore had multiple dream encounters with the old prospector, which he would arise and write down in the middle of the night. Then he would pass them on to Tom Massey, who used Baker's dream experiences in developing the storyline for *The Shovel*.

Baker Fore and Tom Massey have been light-heartedly referred to as the "Barry & Manilow" of self-actualization books—metaphorically speaking, one writes the lyrics and the other adds the melody. Look for their next book entitled: *Nothing Beats R.I.C.H.* In this sequel to *The Shovel*, the characters, Jason Clark,

Joshua Lincoln, Caleb Lincoln, and Alicia Lincoln continue to learn and put into practice the life-changing principles gained through their mystical encounters with the old prospector.

About the Editor

Jessica Bryan

Jessica Bryan is a freelance book editor and author. In 2005, three of the books she edited for the American Academy of Neurology's patient series were nominated for the Foreword Award. In addition to specializing in health-related books for laypersons, she edits self-help, spiritual, and metaphysical books, including three published by Beyond Words Publishing of Portland, Oregon: *Cell-Level Healing*; *JOHN OF GOD: The Brazilian Healer Who's Touched the Lives of Millions*; and *Animals in Spirit*.

Jessica is the author of *PSYCHIC SURGERY AND FAITH HEALING: An Exploration of Multi-Dimensional Realities, Indigenous Healing, and Medical*

Miracles in the Philippine Lowlands (Red Wheel/Weiser/Conari, 2008). She is also the author of *Love is Ageless: Stories About Alzheimer's Disease* (Lompico Creek Press, 2002).

In addition to working in the publishing industry, Jessica does clairvoyant spiritual/health readings and practices a type of energy healing from the Philippines called "Magnetic Healing." She lives in Southern Oregon with Tom Clunie D.C. and can be reached by e-mail to editor@mind.net or telephone: 541-535-6044.

Robert D. Reed Publishers Order Form

> *Call in your order for fast service and quantity discounts!*
> **(541) 347- 9882**

OR order on-line at **www.rdrpublishers.com** *using PayPal.*
OR order by FAX at **(541) 347-9883** *OR by mail:*
Make a copy of this form; enclose payment information:
Robert D. Reed Publishers, 1380 Face Rock Drive, Bandon, OR 97411

Send indicated books to:

Name_____

Address_____

City_____ State _____ Zip _____

Phone: _____ Fax _____ Cell _____

E-Mail _____

Payment by check /_/ or credit card /_/ *(All major credit cards are accepted.)*

Name on card _____

Card Number _____

Exp. Date _____ Last 3-Digit number on back of card _____

		Quantity	Total Amount
The Shovel: Laws for Living by Baker Fore and Tom Massey..............................	$12.95	_____	_____

OTHER BOOKS BY TOM MASSEY:

		Quantity	Total Amount
How Bad Do You REALLY Want It? Getting from Where You Are to Where You Want to Go!	$19.95	_____	_____
The ABC's of Successful Living: Getting What You REALLY Want!...	$9.95	_____	_____
The ABC's of Total Health: Practical Tips for Abundant Living...	$9.95	_____	_____
The ABC's of Effective Leadership: Managing from the Heart..	$9.95	_____	_____
Ten Commitments for Building High Performance Teams...	$11.95	_____	_____
Ten Commitments for Men...................................	$11.95	_____	_____

Quantity of books ordered: _____ Total amount for books: _____

Shipping is $3.50 1st book + $1 for each additional book: Plus postage: _____

FINAL TOTAL: _____